GREEN
VALLEY ROAD

Where "living in the moment" was a sin

E TED GLADUE

COMMONWEALTH BOOKS INC.
New York City 2021

A COMMONWEALTH PUBLICATIONS PAPERBACK
GREEN VALLEY ROAD
This edition published 2021
By Commonwealth Books

Copyright © 2021 by E. Ted Gladue
Published in the United State by Commonwealth Books Inc.,
New York.

Library of Congress Control Number: 2020946520

ISBN: 978-1-892986-21-4 (Trade)

First Commonwealth Books Trade Edition: January 2021

PUBLISHED BY COMMONWEALTH BOOKS, INC.
www.commonwealthbooks@aol.com
www.commonwealthbooksinc.com

Manufactured in the United States of America

This novel is dedicated to
Michael Madden & Michael Lawrence,
two of my former college students
who blessed me with their
lifelong brotherhood

Chapter 1

There really wasn't much green, just small row house lawns and some hedges. No valley, for it sat on high ground in what was called Highland Park. Calling it a "road" sounded nice, but it was more like a "street;" with "road" designation giving it a more suburban claim not really justified by its very geography.

The culture was dominated by the Catholic church where the nuns and priests taught the young that "idleness was the devil's workshop," the opposite of what children in Asia learning *Buddha cultural emphasis with meditation that allows for presence in the "moment," or the sacred present.

Green Valley Road was but a mile up the hill from the last streets of West Philadelphia, so much higher than in centuries past the university of Pennsylvania built its first observatory with a roof that opened to allow it's then advanced telescopes to explore the night skies, located less than about two hundred yards from Green Valley road, sitting on a huge space the size of about ten football fields with a small farm with chickens, cows, horses, and a large orchard with multiple fruit trees, the entire complex surrounded with a tall fence and a forest of trees allowing it a privacy in some mysterious way that few explored. An oasis on a plateau from which on a clear day one could see the statue of William Penn sitting on top of Philadelphia City Hall at 15 and Market Street far below in the city, it fifteen blocks from the Delaware river from which Market Street originated before making its way west and then up the hill to Highland Park, passing the observatory grounds on its route twenty miles west until reaching West Chester Pennsylvania

The fence surrounding this country-like manor in the midst of row home boredom, this young boy did climb, overcoming fears to explore its mystic shadows, territory somehow considered alien by the priests and nuns who occupied the large gray granite stone building just across this narrow street called Saint Lawrence Road, like the 38. parallel that would later separate North and South Korea, a Catholic presence that distrusted this vague and vast land owned by the University of Pennsylvania, nominally a Quaker founded institution. If the priests and nuns knew of my explorations of this property, along with the only pal of mine, Charlie, who would venture with me, they would have severely reprimanded us. It was a no-man's land, it was not Catholic, it was to be ignored as if it did not exist.

But what did exist was the large church property on this side of St. Lawrence Road that towered over the row houses on Green Valley Road beneath the monstrous gray stone buildings whose very existence represented the Roman Catholic Church in all its power and misplaced and paraded majesty over its so called "flock," married couples who believed they were improving lives, the children of Depression era parents entwined as tightly with the church as the exposed gray mortar between thousands of granite stones used to build all the buildings, at one time meticulously laid out on each huge stone by skilled stone masons, just as they did in building European cathedrals, including Notre Dame.

Chapter 2

In looking back, it was surprising, with the now universal knowledge of so many priests world-wide who sexual abused young kids, that none of this happened at St. Lawrence, for us young guys would have discovered attempted abuse if it had occurred; but most of our parish priests were of Irish decent, and we little young alter-boys learned from one another that when the priest put forth his chalice for us to pour the wine over his fingers into the cup, to make sure to pour and pour and pour; even though it was only the six-thirty morning mass, except for some abusive fathers these priests were the first alcoholics that most of us were to experience, though not yet having any idea it was just that. Curious as to why the priests seemed to enjoy the wine they transformed in the blood of Christ during the mass, a few of us alter-boys would drink the red wine before the priests arrived, sometimes leaving us slightly disoriented, and sometimes even tripping, as once I remember my pal Georgie tripping over a step while carrying the wine that spilled all over the priest's gold and white cassock. I say a "few" for actually, George was the only one I had ever seen drinking the wine and when he showed me, there were then two of us, and we were novice fourth graders, so George had me pledge to never reveal our secret to the upper class alter-boys from fifth to eight grade that I actually learned from drinking wine from him.

He was from an Irish family with nine other non-rowhouse kids who lived in a large three story white and green wooden house with wrap around porches on a large tree filled piece of land across the entrance from the Philadelphia Electric golf course whose confidence and worldly stories were related during our six am plus wine drinking sessions.

George was rather short but of sturdy build with a full head of dark wavy hair and large face that appeared chiseled like stone statues I had seen in parks.   He spoke with a great deal of confidence with hand gestures that would have you constantly looking in the directions to which he pointed, before he would bring you back into a closer orbit.   George was the first guy I ever knew who has experienced some sex with a girl, and this was post-WW II when not even the eighth-grade guys were getting any.

And the "any" wasn't much, but here we were down deep in the lower church's heavily stoned and cavernous dimly lit rooms a short time before the priest would arrive with me in complete awe as George described how he was able to kiss these young girls and not just his tongue into their mouths, but, but...I could not believe it, they allowed him to touch their breasts beneath their shirts and sweaters.   Yea? He was quite a natural actor, leaving me hang as he poured himself more of the altar wine before continuing with how he actually got down to the bra, and, unbelievable, the girl allowed him to remove it. I nearly passed out as he told me what a tit looked like and what it felt like in his hands. "The nipples, the nipples," I asked, what were they like, and shook when he described putting his mouth on them, before bang, the door from the rectory opening as the priest would be coming down the steps at any minute and we would be standing still in our black robes and white linen pull-overs, like two little angels, me glad the black robe was loose enough not to expose my young projection.   Word got to me decades later that George fathered twelve children.

Chapter 3

Speaking of children, there were so many on Green Valley Road, which is why most of the fathers never served in WW II, having exemptions because of children or jobs in defense related industries. Life was filled with noise, life was filled with little boys running wild (little girls remained largely indoors), life was filled with the sounds of sports of all sorts being played on the narrow streets and on the large athletic fields and basketball courts whose fence ran up to about ten yards from the rear of our row house.

During summer months the athletic fields, that we simple called the playgrounds, were pulsating with all sorts of games being played by not only children of all ages but grown men of all ages, the center of which was the softball game played on the main field with such intensity that at times fights broke out, broken up quickly before someone got hurt real badly, for some of these guys were bad-asses in their own right like Fred Elmer who was a Pennsylvania state heavyweight wrestling champion with legs as thick as a wild animal, forearms thicker than most men's calf muscles, and a thick neck bulging with veins pulsating in heat and anger; he facing off against a thirty year old Irish fireman named Mac who was most likely the most intense person on the entire playground, whose flaming red hair was only matched by his enraged temper evident not only by his angry words but the skin on his exposed upper body a deep red as if he were on fire. These two facing off against each other was like the Cold War coming to a head, all over whether a pop-up fly ball was either a foul ball or an out. After the game, the two of them would share a cigarette. Athletes smoked then.

Somewhere out there on left field was a basketball court, with a full-court game going on with as much intensity and sporadic anger as with the softball game, playing out with lean tall muscular young men who normally played for the local high schools and universities who more or less invented basketball in the 1940s and 50's; Villanova, Temple, St Joe's, LaSalle, U. of Penn, or what we called the "Big Five," all of whom would have been contenders in today's Final Four scenarios, had it existed at the time, for dozens of all-Americans from these teams ended up in the pros. Guys like Tom Gola, Wilt Chamberlain, Guy Rodgers, Ernie Beck and many more. On a hot summer night many of them would be on this very court fighting for every point as if it were their last championship game.

One end of the court had a severe tilt on its right side as it leaned toward the fence separating the court from the street called Lynn Boulevard, so any shot taken from that corner had to be projected higher than any normal attempt, and few, even the stars, very rarely shot from that right hand western corner of the court. My bedroom widow overlooked this baseball field and the court and bouncing basketballs often woke me up on Saturday mornings sparking me to put on my sneakers, for I truly loved playing basketball and mostly had to sit and watch since neither side choose me over more competent players. But living so close to the court allowed me to spend hours and hours, often into the night hours with no one on the court as I practiced one shot that was difficult to block, even by one much taller guys than me, a shot I learned watching one of Philadelphia's greatest high school players. It was the hook-shot.

The "hook-shot," today normally taken close into the basket, could be shot from this sunken far off corner of the court, but I learned about the shot itself from a guy named Fannon who played for Saint Thomas Moore high school in West Philadelphia, who won many a game with this surprise unorthodox shot from the far corner, one that I practiced for millions of hours, alone, when no one was around, as I said, often in the dark with only the street lights giving me a glimpse of the rim high up and far away as I would hold the ball far out to my right from the corner, so my arm was actually out of bounds though my feet were in bounds and all was legal.

During all the half-court and full-court games I played in I was usually the last kid chosen and during the entire game was ignored and scored no points, just a body to complete the mandatory number of players, many of whom were just terrific players and athletes whom I deeply admired and felt honored just to be on the court with them, for with all this great talent, the scores were very close, with tension, sweat, and tempers rising the closer to the end. When the ball was thrown to me, it was merely to give another player the opportunity to break free so I could pass it back so he could take that jump shot or drive to the basket for the winning score. The first time that I ignored my supportive obligation and drove to the submerged right-hand corner no defender even bothered to chase me, the least capable among the ten on the court. Mistake. With perfect form I launched the ball into a high arc from that far off corner I had secretly named to myself, the "Far East," as all eyes transfixed on its trajectory as it floated and then quietly fell through the medal rim, then switched through the cloth net, winning the game to the surprise of all the players and those watching the game; except me. I knew it would go in.

The reaction? My teammates burst into laughter. The other five guys looked as if they wanted to kill me on the spot. One, out of anger, bounced the ball so hard against the ground it flew out over the fence onto the boulevard before a car ran over it, boom, and killed it. "Who was watching that asshole," one yelled. "What the fuck," three others yelled. One guy even walked over to me as if he wanted to punch me; but, by that time my weight-lifting had given me a strong body, and no one had bullied me in quite some time, for the few who tried, and used to knock the shit out of me in the old days, I decked and bloodied, so I was spared.

After that, I was usually chosen to play with a side that Jack Gallop, one of most respected guys on the court would select me, he mischievously feeding me the ball at crucial times of the game, knowing I would drive to that far right corner, and in spite of tall very good players covering me, pushing me, fouling me, bingo: I became a threat. Jack loved it, and would laugh his ass off, and referred to that hook shot for many years.

Chapter 4

During those years I became a good football player, street fighter, and boxer; but it was not until my four year military enlistment that my basketball talents improved, playing with so many of my black brothers, I learned more moves than any of my old pals in our all-white neighborhood ever developed, so when I returned home to this very court, I often bested even those younger than me who played for all the great local universities.

Our neighborhood did have physical boundaries that resided somewhat vaguely in our minds with the eastern boundary being the property of the University of Pennsylvania with the Frankenstein like observatory and the western boundary just across the from the basketball court sitting on the corner of West Chester Pike and Lynn Boulevard, a large one story building on about five acres of grounds with large lawns and tall trees of every variety through which long black shinny vehicles slowly entered on a winding driveway, a few parking in an open space, others entering the rear of the building when the large garage doors opened to discretely allow them entrance, as spooky to us kids as the mysterious observatory at the eastern boundary, for our young minds had a difficult time processing that our basketball court overlooked a funeral home called "Donahue," for we understood nothing about death for our parents were young and I can't remember any household who had grandparents living with them. We did not know death, but would learn more about it over the decades as some of our parents died, for Donahue's would eventually bury nearly every parent on Green Valley Road, and beyond. But for now, death and eternity were not understood nor was it on the minds of any of us, only how to get the ball into the basket and win the game. In fact, as we looked at each other, we expected none of our guys would ever change, ever get old or age; just continue to play basketball and smile, laugh, and live forever. When any of us looked at Green Valley Road we did not see houses, we saw families; those living in those red brick structures defined what the brick and mortar was, a living thing that would always be that family now living in that space, forever, as far as our young consciousnesses could fathom.

The southern boundary of our neighborhood was easy to distinguish with the two huge tracks of land that made up two golf courses, one private and one a public course, the latter perhaps two or three times the size of the private one for the employees of the Philadelphia Electric Company whose southern border ran smack up against the playground and about thirty yards from my row house front door. The only problem, was a high metal fence topped with sharp barbed wire with "no trespassing" signs just beneath the medal military looking support rods through which the barbed wire passed, with the rods and wire angled toward the playground, making it very difficult for anyone to climb over without getting caught up and cut with the razor sharp medal tips of the wire.

But for some strange reason, this menacing barrier's physical reality went almost unchallenged, for most of the kids had no desire to climb it or explore the beautiful rolling green of the fairways, streams, and small forests of trees throughout this very special piece of nature preserved under the guise of a golf course. Except, for me.

In my early explorations to escape the tyranny of my parents, teaching nuns, and neighborhood bullies, I found that at the juncture where the security fence met the long iron fence running above the stone wall behind all the houses whose rears faced the golf course, the row houses across from Green Valley Road on what was Academy Lane, the few strains of sharp wire could be violated by carefully placing one leg over the wire at a time, being careful not to catch my young balls on the wire before jumping ten feet or more to the ground inside the golf course, and freedom.

I knew of no other kid besides myself who successfully climbed into this paradise of nature. One of my first projects was to build a primitive platform tree house high up on the thick branches of a magnificent large gray oak tree from where I could watch the golfers on the fairways and tees, and they could not see me. After the course closed and the only life on the fairways were the hundreds of birds landing and feeding, the golf pro, way down below near the practice greens, would hit dozens of balls up the hill attempting to reach a tee from which the golfers during the day would hit off on their way to the third green.

For some strange reason, I have not, even to this day figured out; I would lay flat on the ground beneath bushes at the top of the hill watching the pro down below, a tall thin man who always wore the same off-white cap as he hit ball after ball up in my direction, a few even rolling a few feet from me. Early on, I would grab only those balls near me, but soon would reach out beyond the bushes to grab the few balls within reach hoping he would not see me, and later retreat up into my secret tree-hut and store them in a hole in the tree. The pro had a system worked out where one of his assistants would drive a cart with some sort of scooping capability up onto the fairway in the morning to retrieve the balls, including those that had rolled out of sight beneath "my" bushes.

Now, perhaps it would take a psychiatrist to figure out my motivation, for I had somehow come to like and admire this lonely thin figure of a pro down below, I began to ever so timidly at first, emerge from beneath the bushes and reach out to grab the balls easy to reach before crawling back beneath the bushes, but before long I was running five yards, then ten, then twenty yards down the fairway grabbing balls and putting them into a small bucket I carried before racing back to the sanctuary of my bushes, and as you might guess before long the pro was waving his club in anger and even from this distance could hear him yelling something until I again disappeared beneath the bushes at the top of the fairway, and after a time, he would resume hitting balls thinking the kid at the top had run off, and then I would reappear, now running perhaps forty yards down the hill grabbing balls he had hit with smaller seven or nine irons, until the man completely lost it, for I could hear his curse words and see him waving his golf club in the air as if wishing he could strike me with it as I sprinted back up the hill, disappearing into the bushes before climbing up into my secret tree hut with another bucket of golf balls as the pro, now huffing and puffing from his forced march up the hill stood within the small forest looking in every direction for the kid who violated his ritual, not thinking to look up into the large oak tree, where I sat with total satisfaction that I beat at least one grown-up, for all those who tortured my existence on the lands outside this small gift of nature.

Yea, it felt like only existence on the other side of the wall and fence; for I faced a heavy-handed father, nasty insulting demeaning Catholic nuns with punishments ranging from being trapped in a detention after school let out to physical pain from rulers and window poles smashed down on my head and body, the embarrassment of being held back a year in school, for as told to my mother, "being the dumbest kid the nun ever taught," while other dumb kids mothers bribed nuns with cakes and pies, when Mom did not even bother to gain some favor by informing that her older sister was at the time a Franciscan teaching nun in a semi-cloistered order in South Philadelphia, older insecure boys who punched and kicked and called names that to this day I will not tell anyone. So, the formattable physical barrier to prevent the peasants from Green Valley Road to step onto the green carpets of the golf course kept all the local boys out, except me.

On one summer evening I brought with me a pair of military binoculars that my U.S. Army uncle George had left allowing me to get a close-up view of the golf pro from whom I had been stealing the golf balls. When focusing in on him something changed within my heart for he had this sad look on his face, a look of loneliness, eyes that this powerful military instrument enabled me to see as if I were just a few feet away from him, and I suddenly felt something that I only felt with a few of my wonderful uncles who always treated me with love and respect when we visited them on Sundays. That night I waited till near nightfall when he walked back up to the pro shop and after climbing back up to my tree-fort and retrieving nearly three buckets of balls I walked down to the spot from which he hit and left them with a note: "Sorry."

Chapter 5

After that I ventured down beyond the clubhouse and parking lots discovering a little stream whose waters were so clear, clean, and cool that I took off my shoes and submerged my feet till the stones on the bottom sent impulses past my skin to my small foot bones, massaging as mother nature does, sending currents of peace all the way up my nervous system to my brain, accompanied by soothing sounds as the water coming out of the underground pipe dropped just a few inches into the stream now flowing around my leg muscles, water splashing upon water, me then pulling out my little thing to hear a new sound, my pee hitting the water, as primitive as an animal in the wild.

Then I began to discover living things in and close to the stream. Small fish, tadpoles, little things covered with shells as if in the ocean; and along the banks turned up rocks with unbelievable variety of colors were tadpoles, and even frogs; never before had I come in such close contact with nature, and what did I do? As in a family, the abused become abuser. For once I had a power over others. The small fish I tried, but could not catch but I could collect the shelled things and with a rock in my hand smash them to bits, found a way to trap the tadpoles with my hanky and throw them onto the bank before smashing them with the same rock, now acquiring some blood, and felt so accomplished, like a hunter, when capturing a small frog who suffered the same fate. My pride and joy were in finding a small snake under a rock and smashing its fucking head like a tadpole. I was having so much fun, or satisfaction? I returned every day for a month working my way down the stream, killing everything I could get my hands on.

Then one day I reached the fence that separated this private course from the public one called Cobbs Creek Golf Course, it of course having "No Trespassing" signs all over it, plus "Danger" signs, for beyond the fence was an elevated rail line called the PNW, the fastest train in all of Philadelphia for it was powered electrically, with what was known as the "third rail," a deadly live metal rail running alongside the train tracks that would electrocute any living thing that came in contact with it. Parents and teachers in the area told stores of children who ignored the warning signs and brought their dogs so close they were "electrocuted," burnt to death; and, only related in hushed tones by mothers with tears in their eyes, of several children who died trying to cross the tracks in order to get to the golf course or Cobbs Creek that ran through the course on its meanderings to the far off Delaware River.

Here I was six or seven years old standing at the base looking up at the track and the stones upon which they sat with the hot summer sun glistening off both the tracks and the deadly rail beneath them but all I could think of was the forest of trees beyond and could hear the rushing waters of a stream as it fell from a waterfall beyond. I felt like a hunter, and wanted to hunt and kill; for I was discovering a new power, like the power others had over me.

Behind me, all the fears I would encounter every day; in front of me, no fear, not even this third rail, in spite of seeing a dead and burnt fox and a dead and burnt muskrat, as I slowly placed my feet over one rail and then the other, all the while starring with much intensity upon the deadly rail just a foot near my last stepping foot to clear it all and onto the rocks and then the earth beneath. For some reason, my pulse remained the same, calm, and as I began to walk down toward the sound of the water I could hear the whistle of a train in the distance and as I turned to look up was surprised at how quickly it had come, speeding past so fast my hair was blowing into my eyes, and my ears sort of crackled from the pressure of the winds.

The golf course itself was a full football field and a half away from this new jungle like forest I had just entered with a small river-like Cobbs Creek meandering through it as if in a jungle with so many waterfalls created by beavers allowing one to cross over from one side to another every so often, exotic birds making sounds high up in the trees as nature's symphony blending with the splashing of waterfalls and flapping leaves on trees and tropical like palms, a world away from all the seriousness of life far above this new found wonderland, seemingly void of all humans, and so wild that on this very first contact a deer bolted from behind some ferns and jumped into a shallow crossing of the creek with the speed of a trolley car on West Chester Pike hopping between the trees on the far side as the white tip of its tail disappeared into the forest, my jaw dropping and eyes wide in utter amazement.

When I returned the next day, I carried my prized Christmas present, my bee-bee pump gun, filled with pellets, for here again I felt in control of things beyond me, with no fear of anything in this environment. I soon learned what a good shot I was with being able to shoot so many birds even high up in the trees, and after kicking over so many rocks and stones shot those in nature I hated the most, snakes of all sizes and colors, and when none were to found, lizards and salamanders of more colors than a rainbow, and soon discovered that when throwing bread crumbs I had brought from home upon the water I could shoot some of the larger fish that swam to the surface to feed. My dream was to shoot and kill a beaver, or a deer; to kill, to kill, to torture as I did the salamanders. In essence, I was inflicting pain, rather than receiving pain. This heart of nature so close to my horrible row-house environment now became abused, by one who knew only abuse.

Then one day I stumbled upon two young guys in the midst of my forest; one, at the base of a tree the other who had climbed nearly twenty feet up who was screaming to the one below: " The bag, the bag;" as the one at the base of the tree opened a large cloth bag just before a shimmering flashing image feel into it, a large tree snake.

It turned out the two were twins who happened to live just a half mile from me, about seven or eight years older quickly became mentors to this young explore/hunter, who had much to learn. On that introductory day I immediately offered them the use of my bee-bee gun to shoot the snake they had captured. I will never forget the expressions on their bewildered faces, which spoke more than their words, for they were not much about expressing themselves with language, perhaps the reason they spent all their time in the woods in quiet solitude communicating with a sign language only they understood. Without any words of recrimination toward me they simple took the large snake from the bag and each of them allowed it to wrap itself around their hands, then their wrists, then their forearms as I stood in fear at first, and then total rapture as this wild snake wrapped around and slid upon the one brother's skin till it reached his upper arms before it sort of laid back and lifted its head, now pointed at his face, as if to strike as the two of them just froze into a eye to eye contact, with the snake's head remaining in a slightly back holding position like a deadly snake about to strike.

Minutes later the snake more or less voluntarily slid in a bag held by one of the brothers as if they were taking in a field mouse. From there I followed them on their journey as they walked along the stream throwing treats upon the waters as beavers appeared out of nowhere in a flash to devour those pieces on the surface of the stream, and most amazing the beautiful wild birds I had been shooting scooped down upon the ground as they scattered seeds upon the leaves and grasses, and then we three sat on a earthen plot of ground as blue/green clean waters rushed beneath and past us with accompanying winds cleansing our lungs; when, as if on script small fish the size of ones I had killed, swam into the deep waters as my two new pals threw feed upon the waters as the fish swarmed in hunger and trust.

In silence, as always with the two of them, we sat for quite some time with nature's sounds of windblown leaves and grasses alongside the creek, birds singing after returning up high from feeding just a few feet from where we sat, splashing sounds as water washed over rocks and beaver falls, in this valley beneath all the noise and congestion of neighborhoods of rowhouses surrounding the huge granite buildings of the church, I had met the first environmentalists of my life, who without words bonded me to nature with a new respect, now seeing a vulnerability in nature I had not understood before, and that my attacks on nature reflected my personal vulnerability, a behavior that would change somewhat from this moment on.

Chapter 6

When home up in my tree-fort I thought much about what I was learning from the brothers and began a small dairy trying to express what as an adult I would later call perceptions, but then just confusion, and the thinking emanating from this confusion carried over to my home when my mother would chastise me for just looking out a window and daydreaming, and a major problem arose when in school, far removed physically, emotionally, spiritually from sitting in the woods by the stream.

The gray granite stone walls of St. Lawrence school were no different than prisons up-state, and the nuns were not much different in temperament and personality than guards, perhaps more dangerous, for grown prisoners at least have a handle on who they are as human beings; whereas us children are still captive to what grown-ups and authorities think of us and what they project onto us. I was assigned to a seat in the back of our class near a rear window allowing me to get a glimpse of a tree outside which opened my young mind to what I was learning in the forest by the stream in the valley below, as I was beginning to understand what my new friends were trying to teach me about the interconnectedness of all creatures and their environments in nature, of course not in these terms, but in my young mind, I could almost hear those leaves outside the window blowing their sounds with the chirping of birds and smells coming off the stream...then...BANG...crashing down on my head...cracking my skull, my head hitting the desk temporarily knocking me unconscious, seeing lights, feeling pain, then my head being jerked back with a clump of my hair in the nun's hand...her screaming...."What are you doing starring out the window and not looking at you book?? Over and over again... her face now but inches from mine, her eyes with more hate than I had yet seen in my few years on this planet. "So you like it out there young man when you should be paying attention to what I am writing on the front board, or looking at your book; you are the worst student in this class, and you will serve an after school detention for two weeks. Then maybe you will learn to pay attention and stare out windows. For day- dreaming is the devil's workshop.... Yes, never forget that: day-dreaming is the devil's workshop," as she brought that dam wooden clicker cracking down on the top of my head, again. "Daydreaming is the devil's workshop," a phrase I would hear from nuns for my nine years of Catholic grammar school; perhaps why not one student ever became a poet.

I really had only one friend who was a "daydreamer," his name was Charlie. We spent a lot of time in what we called "the jungles" along Cobbs Creek that ran through both golf courses, and we were the only kids that we knew of who explored the no-man's land across from the church property with the fruit trees, farms, and most intriguing of all, the Observatory, that to us resembled a building out of a Frankenstein movie with its spooky façade rounded off like an upside down cup with old dirty reddish stones, the few visible windows blacken deep dark except for a slight, hardly visible, yellow light slightly pulsating with an eerie glow. The only entrance door had a large black heavy medal knocker hanging at face level for a grownup, a child having to reach up.

One night there was no moon but the skies were blinking with stars and all sorts of white flashing things up high in the black of the universe and since we knew that on this night someone was inside for once, we simultaneously reached up, grabbed the heavy knocker, lifted it as high as we could, and smashed it against the small medal base plate; once, than twice, before simultaneously stepping back a few feet, without communicating to each other a slight fear that we may have overstepped a boundary, for we could detect the heavy breathing in each other, and then: bam, the opening of the heavy door nearly knocked us off our feet as it swung open, as we both jumped slightly at the sight of the image of a man standing before us, just an image, for the lights behind him were enough to cause us to blink before getting a focus on a man before us, an older man with long white hair and a beard to match.

"Hello boys, come on in," with a soft kind voice bringing us instant relief, especially upon looking into his smiling face as he so casually led us to a black medal staircase with the two of us following him as he ascended the stairs, "be careful boys, just take one step at a time." The interior of the place was as dark and mysterious as the outer walls suggested but with trust in our young hearts we followed the old man up till were face to face with this large telescope that reached up to the opening in the rounded ceiling high above allowing us to view the very heavens we had been in awe of before entering.

The old man informed us, one at a time, to sit on a small stool as he brought the slender end of the eyeglass contraption to our right eye, placing our right hands on it, as he made adjustments turning several knobs here and there, and WOW... never before in my young life, did I ever view the magnificence of the night sky's mysteries as at this very moment. Of course, this telescope had been built in the 1930s and could not compare in any way to today's technology that has even photographed a black hole millions of light years away, but for two kids in the early 1940s to experience this was truly a life changing event, one that we shared and talked about for years afterwards, long after the Observatory, the farms, and the entire area was sold, destroyed, and replaced by a huge athletic facility as pedestrian as the rest of the row home neighborhood. When either of us tried to tell the nuns, who taught us about our experiences we were immediately not only shut down, but threatened: "If the priests knew you were on that property you would both be in big trouble." Such was life in those days of conservative Catholic insular thinking.

Chapter 7

Not only did these nuns discourage any learning outside their narrow education and myopic view of the world but would try and crush any child who was different, and I mean "crush." The violence by a nun I alluded to earlier upon my young self could have affected me my entire life, for she was not only a bad teacher, violent, and sadistic; but had a power that she should have never possessed, the power to keep me in her class for not just the one year, but two. Think, how a child deals with time? A year to a child is like ten years to an adult. In looking back, especially having studied psychiatry at Mt Sinai medical school in New York City, this nun had serious mental problems and no one came to my defense as she beat me with window poles and heavy yardsticks, kept me locked up in a room after all the other kids left after school, and the nightmare: left me down, meaning all my friends went on to fifth grade while I was humiliated and kept back for an entire year. And my parents, said nothing, except that something was wrong with me. This nun, Sister Charles Marie whom we called "Battleship Marie," was trying to murder my spirit. I will never forget the day of this decision, walking out of the school into the late afternoon school-yard, all the kids had rejoiced and left, and I was all alone, so confused, so afraid, so embarrassed, in fear of going home to my parents who never took my side and never stood up for me, and knowing how other kids were going to make fun of me for being so stupid, which they did, during the entire summer.

Returning to school the following September was like being put in solitary confinement for the mistreatment and violence continued, the afterschool confinement, the humiliation in front of the other students, the anger and condemnation of my mother and father that never let up, punches to my body and head by older students who could sense my vulnerability and knew none of the nuns would believe me if I told them I was being bullied. It was the longest year of my life at the time, and forever thereafter. To this day I can't remember how old I was? Fourth grade? But this humiliation continued for four more years, up till eighth-grade, and then an amazing transformation took place, which I will writer about later, for now I want to skip a decade or so, beyond high school, four years of military service, four years of college, to this story.

It was all for extensive purposes, confirmed by the Chairman of the History department at Villanova University, Dr Henry Rofinot, a professor of history; as least that is what he so kindly called me, even though I was only on a graduate teaching fellowship , and if I may add, rated as one of the top professors by all seventy of my students, against all the tenured professors in the department at the time. One day, a full-time professor asked me if I would do him a favor and teach a class for him on a Saturday morning in downtown Philadelphia, the subject, 19 and 20 century German history, that he was unable to meet. I accepted.

When I arrived I was very surprised that the class was made up of nuns, the same order of nuns who taught me in grammar school, their hoods and blackness causing me momentary shock, me, who had experience death and combat during my four year military service, facing a past I thought was dead.

Always the professional, I opened my briefcase on the desk, looked up and introduced myself in a kind and friendly manner. But there, in the front row, exactly in front of my desk, was the bitch: Sister Charles Maria, old "Battleship Marie," for these nuns took years and years to get their degrees.

My first inclination was to walk over, and demand this child molester to leave my class. But, now being a professor, I ignored my enraged instincts, and went on to give one of the best lectures in my young life, which to my surprise, most of the nuns respected enough to actually clap at the end of the two-hour presentation, for I worked every intellectual corner of the subject, having read about 25 books on the subject as well as my own personal research while stationed in Germany. I was good and I was hot. Several nuns came up to tell me they had never experience a professor's presentation as mine. "Battleship Maria" merely slid away, sneakily retreating to the rear of the room without ever looking back, as I watched, being careful not to give in to my animal instincts that were screaming at me to throw "the fucking textbook at the bitch." God forbid.

But most interesting; I could not wait to tell my little old Irish mother what had transpired, expecting a big smile and perhaps, a pat on the back; as an Italian, Jewish, Latino, Afro-American mother would have done: instead, she shocked me. "Oh, the poor nun, it is taking her so long to get her degree." Her response drove me to a local bar; but, it was not much unlike decades later, long after I was divorced from my only wife, and my mother was a widow having dinner at my home, me treating her as if she were a Queen; after a few drinks she would begin to jab me in the arm with her fingers: "what is wrong with you? Why did you get divorced?" Mom, I would say, at least I am not a child molester, like all those priests. Mom would respond: "Oh, the poor priests, it happened so long ago" Such is justice from an Irish mother...but I still love ya Mom.

Chapter 8

A year before this nasty brutal fourth grade nun, I had my first, somewhat confused, attraction to a member of the opposite sex; a sweet little third grade girl with pig-tails, big blue eyes, a face that never allowed a smile, and a nose that always seemed to be held up as if " I am unapproachable." Whenever I tried to talk with her, she merely turned her head away from me as if I did not exist. She sat behind me in class and several times I turned around and tried to get her attention, each time she simply raised her hand, and bingo; the nun yelled at me to "turn around in your desk young man."

At the end of the day us students had to retrieve out coats from a very long narrow closet, of which I always made sure that my coat was near hers at the deep end of the closet; and one day I waited until she was more or less unable to leave for I was in her way; at which point I leaned my head forward and kissed her on the lips, at which point she screamed so loud that the nun came crashing into the closet to save the young damsel. I spent five days in detention.

One day, as I turned around, she actually allowed a conversation between us, and I told her that I was going to join the Marines and go and fight in the Pacific if she did not "like me." She just looked at me as if I did not exist. On Halloween that year I was told by my classmate that he had been invited to her home for a costume party, and not being invited, I was sad. But I told my mother I had been invited and her and my younger sister dressed me up as a girl; then spend so much time with make-up after fitting me with a dress, stockings and high heels etc. dam, did I look like a broad.

When I got to the party I was greeted by the girl and father at the front door, and she had no idea it was me as both she and her father let me in. We played many games, one of which was popular at the time called "spin the bottle," where boys and girls would sit in a circle with an empty coke bottle in the center which someone would spin, and when it stopped, whomever it pointed at, would be required to spin it again, and whomever it pointed at, they had to kiss. Except, that is, if it were of the same sex, God forbid, no one thought of that at the time.

There I sat, unbeknownst to her, across from my love, and could not keep my eyes off of her, for her costume was that of an elf, and she was so cute. I don't think, or remember, any sexual drives at work here, just my first infatuation with the opposite sex, and after so many spins of the bottle, I finally got lucky...bingo....my spin, and it pointed at my little elf; she smiled for the first time, then I crawled over and kissed her on the lips, and at that very second she recognized me, screamed, sat up and ran to her father, who proceeded to throw me out the fucking front door as if I were a thief. I did try to steal a kiss from his little third grade daughter. And there I was, out on the street, walking home in my long dress and high heels, never to be kissed by a girl for the next twelve years, when one of my Irish pals would "give" me his girl, who loved him. But that is another story, for later.

Chapter 9

Jobs. My father got me out working very young. Most of the kids on Green Valley Road did not work, nor where they pressured to work. Most of the fathers worked in places where they wore suit and ties and carried themselves as if they had important high paid employment, which few did, but carried themselves as if they did, and were so self-conscience of status, for mostly all came from working class families who struggled during the Great Depression, whose own fathers were often laborers in factories and industrial work places in south, north , or west Philadelphia, for in the 1930s Philadelphia was quite a productive city with thousands of opportunities for employment for row house working class families from which Green Valley Road fathers came, but having moved just beyond the borders of South or West Philadelphia, a mile up the hill, were attempting to escape not just their working class roots, but the very images of what that meant. My father, on the other hand, was proud of his hard-earned money from his factory job and made no pretense to be anything else in spite of blending in at Church on Sunday mornings dressed in impressive three-piece suits and ties, looking more like a banker than a factory worker. Dad would work an eight-hour night shift at the textile plant as a "loom fixer," that today would be classified as a mechanical engineer, for it did take a lot of brains to look at a flaw in a printed fabric or rug and figure out how to fix the machine, or loom, in order to correct the problem. I remember times when three or four men from the factory would come sit with my father in our living room discussing how to fix the flaw in the loom, for evidently, he was one of the best at his trade, and the bosses and other fixers were desperate to find a solution, which my father evidently did most of the time, but the men did not stay long after, for Dad did not drink nor keep liquor in our home. And as I learned very young at our summer factory parties throughout Philadelphia, most of these men were heavy drinkers. I still remember the tension and quiet tears of wives and children in our car after these all-day events as my sober non-drinking father drove them safely home after being abandoned by a drunken husband and father.

My Dad worked two jobs; for with only a couple hours sleep after a night shift he would rise early and paint the outside of the houses on our row house block, dressed in beat-up overalls and painters hats he climbed up and down his heavy wooden two story ladders painting the brick houses wooden windows, frames and doors on the homes of men who even on weekends remained in their executive looking attire, my father reminding them of where they came from, and I was even conscious as I grew older how some of these fathers and wives tried to look down on my dad, as beneath them; but, Dad did not give a dam about that, he just took their money, and funnily, we always had the newest shiny big car on Green Valley Road, and we were the only family that took summer vacations, and our house was the first property on Green Valley Road to have the mortgage paid in full.

But me, I hated work. But Dad found me work when I was younger than I can remember. In those days milk, bread, and newspapers all got delivered to the homes; and there I was helping the milk man on his route before the sun came up delivering fresh milk picking up the used bottles on mornings before global warming when freezing temperatures combined with heavy snows and icy concrete steps for in Highland Park mostly all the homes were above street level, many very high, and I only got paid about two dollars a day that began at four or five am and ended earlier enough to allow me to change clothes and get to school on time. Carrying those bottles up and down the steps was hard and somewhat dangerous; but the bread man would try and make it fun by tossing the bread to me as if it were a football expecting me to not just walk up the steps, but to run up them. And being a bad asthmatic, winter mornings were tough on me, especially before modern medicine offered prevention. I can't remember what happened to the two dollars the milk or bread man would pay me, for Mom took it from me to pay for school expenses, and a few cents reward for me to go to a movie or sometimes buy some candy. But my father was happy; for the bread man would give him a free pie or cake, and the milkman would give him some free eggs. What I hated most of all, was getting up so early.

But these jobs did help in one way, my young legs got very strong running up and down all the row house steps, sufficiently preparing me for my next job, caddying at the many golf and country-club courses in the suburbs of Philadelphia with hills that were tough to climb with two heavy leather bags filled with many many heavy golf clubs owned by the doctors and lawyers who got cheap labor for two dollars and fifty cents a bag, most never even giving a tip at the end of a grueling eighteen hole course with hills so steep, and these were the days before golf carts when everyone had to walk. Not all twelve year old boys had the leg and body strength to carry two very heavy leather bags up and up and up, for eighteen holes, all the while putting up with the petty demands from men whose athletic skills were so bad and they swung the clubs so awkwardly that it took a great deal of will-power not to laugh.

There came a time when the golf teaching pros took notice of certain young boys who had not only the strength and endurance to carry the bags but had the presence to remain nearly invisible, like a shadow in responding to requests for clubs and balls. The pros did not employ a kid who was huffing and puffing, nor annoying in any way that distracted from his teaching the game of golf. I became a favorite of the teaching pros at a very young age, perhaps late in my twelve year, and I absorbed all they were trying to teach the awkward doctors and lawyers, unlike my total rejection of the failed teaching methods of the Catholic nuns, their teaching stuck, and when back home I would climb over the private golf course fence facing the front door of our row house with my seven and nine irons and a putter on those dreamy late summer evenings whenever the pro went home and put into practice all I was learning from the teaching pros; I could soon hit a seven iron like a pro.

But more importantly at the time, the same prideful doctors and lawyers made sure to seek me out to carry their bags, for they leaned on me for knowledge: of which clubs to use at every juncture of their 18-hole struggle to not look like a fool. It did not take me long to judge their abilities, strengths, and weaknesses, of course, not as good as the pro teaching them a week before, but we caddies got to know the courses so well and what it took to clear a hill, a fairway, a clump of trees, a pond or creek; and combined with being able to judge the weaknesses of these awkward rich men, and how to advise them on which clubs to use, anticipating a successful, or at least, not an embarrassing swing of the club, but to just hit the fucking ball in the right direction. It's called "clubbing" a golfer around a course. And with all their prideful personalities, they needed a kid with skills, who at the same time, seemed dense enough not to absorb the reality of what he was witnessing. For never once, in all those years, did any of those bastards ever reach out with a kind word of thanks, for "clubbing" their awkward asses through the eighteen holes of golf, on Main Line courses of Philadelphia blue bloods and the newly rich and professional.

Chapter 10

By my sixteenth birthday I could most likely hit a seven-iron shot as good as any pro with strong hands and upper arms that no man could or would ever beat me in arm wrestling. Even though I lost interest in golf; years later, after serving four years in the military and four years of college, and now a young professor in a Master's degree program, I was hired as a pool manager and swimming coach, thanks to Villanova's swimming coach, one of the greatest swimmers and coaches in Philly, Ed Geisz, who with Joe Vidore at LaSalle high school had created the now accepted butterfly kick. The new job was at what was Flowertown country Club, owned by George Fassio, who was considered the golfer with the greatest iron shot in all of professional golf.

George, or Mr. Fassio as I called him, would hit golf balls for hours behind the swim club, and as often as I could, I would watch him, hour after hour; till one day he recognized me as his pool manager, and then, there I was: with a 7 iron in my hand, as he watched me take swing after swing. I will never forget, this great man's complements of my ability with a 7 iron... but hey, that's all history. But it all began with the sweat and toil of a twelve-year-old boy lugging bags to make a buck.

Back on Green Valley Road a lot was changing. I did survive the two years in fourth grade with the child abuser of a nun called "Battleship Marie," and all the humiliations during fifth, sixth, seventh, and eighth-grades, emerging from these years with no respect, from most, including my parents, and had no idea what to expect going into high school, which demanded that I attend a Catholic one, and that one was down the hill from Highland Park on West Chester Pike till it became Market street at 63 street, running beneath the elevated trains till it reached 49 street. It was the infamous West Philadelphia Catholic High School for Boys, a breeder of champs, in football, basketball, track, and anything competitive. During eighth grade my St. Lawrence team won what was called the CYO championship in football. I was on that team, having begun the season as the starting fullback, but on the first play from scrimmage, on the opening day of the season, I took the ball on a hand-off into the line and sprained by ankle so badly that I was unable to play for four games, and when returning, was reduced to a substitute guard and played very little. I was humiliated. Our championship dinner was addressed by the coach of West Catholic, a former Eagles player, (Kearnens) and he urged all of us champions to try out for West Catholic when we would begin in the Fall of 1950. On the way home from the banquet I told my father that I was going to try out: he said: "You never even played much at St Lawrence, how are you going to Play for West Catholic?"

And he had a strong point; for across from our home, no more than 100 yards, on Academy Lane, lived one of the greatest running backs in all of Philadelphia football history, Charlie Alburtis, the very first hero of my life, whom I would see in church on the mornings of his big games, walking up to receive communion from the priest, my 11 year old eyes fixated on him as if her were Babe Ruth, thinking to myself: "what is he thinking."

After our championship banquet, before I left with my father, all the players were in great spirit, slapping each other on the back and smiling with such confidence for they just knew they were going to be the next stars at West Catholic. Not one of my fellow players even recognized my existence, nor said goodbye to me upon leaving, ever after my going out of my way to extend a goodbye. I was a nothing, to all of them, including my father, as the walk home showed.

But the summer before high school changed a lot of reality. My next door neighbor's oldest son, Allen Eisenhuth who was on active duty with the Air Force where he served as a physical rehabilitation specialist to wounded combat guys. He talked my reluctant father into buying me a set of weights for Christmas, and there in our low ceiling darkened basement taught me how to build my body, and then more, how to use my fists, using boxing skills unknow in our environment at the time.

Within four months, I walked up from those basement training exercises and out into onto Green Valley Road on a May morning with confidence, without any fear, that I carry to this very day, as I did on the athletic fields that entire summer.

My first physical encounter that summer was with a systemic bully name joey Walters who lived approximately ten row houses east of us on the same south side of Green Valley Road, who would go out of his way to torment me, as he attempted to do one day when I was throwing a football back and forth with another kid next to the stone wall to avoid being near any of the others who were playing baseball, basketball, or sitting playing different card games on the road above our heads. We chose this spot precisely to avoid any others but all of a sudden Joey Walters was standing beside us with a wise guy smirk on his face as he stepped in front of my friend and intercepted the ball, my ball, the cheap one I had gotten for Christmas but polished it time and time again with shoe polish so it would look more official, as I had done an hour before.

Joey took the ball over the granite stone wall next to the steps leading up to the road in front of the school where a card game was going on and began to rub the ball against rough edges of the stone cutting and slicing until it nearly cut through to the bladder. What transpired next was not just viewed by dozens in that playground that day, but became legendary.

Without any thought or plan, I simply grabbed Joey's shirt at the chest with one hand and with the other grabbed him between the legs with not just his pants, but his balls, as I lifted his entire body up to my chest, and then above me head like a barbell, took about four steps in reaching the hard stone like macadam surface of the basketball court before slamming him to its surface with a sickening thud that echoed off the granite school above vibrating all the way to the golf course fence fifty yards or more to the north, everyone that day in earshot just froze, some in awe, some surprised, but all knowing exactly what happened. Ted would never again be a guy you could bully or even mess with, and this new reputation spread far and wide, all the way down the hill to West Philly. But, as with gun-slingers in the old wild west, fools would challenge me, to their misfortune, as one after another of the bullies who tormented me for years, tested me with insulting and demeaning provocations. But never again, on Green Valley Road, would any bully transgress my being, nor any other kid bullied anywhere in Highland Park, as several long time nasty bastards quickly learned when they again bullied the only Jew in our neighborhood, Benny Gulp, me coming out from behind some bushes seeing the terrified look on Benny's face, that quickly changed as I took two of the bullies down with kicks and punches as the third one ran as if his pants were on fire, Benny now smiling and in near complete misbelief that here was his only friend in our Catholic centric neighbor, himself a victim of the bullies, had miraculously transformed his body and mind, and came to Benny being attacked, again, for simple being a Jew.

Chapter 11

When you were a kid on Green Valley Road our parents taught us to respect every adult, which we did by rote, but many of the adults appeared mysterious in some way, ways that youngsters could not begin to unravel, even though we tried in our small innocent ways. For one, there was Mr. Farnesworth who lived about five or six row houses east of us, the father of about three or four children, whom no one knew much about, except that he was gone a lot for he worked in Washington D.C. for the Department of Defense or the Pentagon, or one of those institutions we knew little about.

To a young boy he looked like the movie actor Van Heflin, tall, lean, with a thick had of brown hair, huge suspicious-looking brown eyes, who seemed to where the same baggy brown suit with a matching brown tie and white shirt, a man who seldom spoke to neighbors, or anyone, but soon came under a great deal of suspicion and ostracism as a result of his drunken rages that could be heard for nearly a hundred yards in any direction from that small little row house beneath the church property.

Everyone tried to ignore his madness, even after his wife and children would leave the house, frantically climbed into the family car, and drove off to, wherever? For in those desperate moments Mr. Fransworth was not only ranting and raving with a voice, as I said, could be heard for hundreds of yards away, the fuel for such rage, bottle after bottle of whiskey, when emptied, was thrown down the steps leading from the row house kitchen to the basement, smashing with such dramatic clarity that even the nuns in their granite stoned building but a football field away must have been able to hear. The smashing of glass on concrete was nothing less than frightening to the ears of not only children in other row houses, but other adults, who never spoke of it, nor condemned it, for many of them had just emerged from depression era homes in south, north, and west Philly with fathers who had been damaged by the Great Depression, in spirit and soul, and drank the alcohol in equally heavy quantities that many recognized in the cries of pain, anger, and broken glass, coming from a neighbor they did not know much about, but said not much about, and for some strange reason, never spoke about nor condemned, as if it did not happen. These men, fathers, faithful church goers and ushers who all dressed like Wall Street bankers or lawyers, with kind faces and friendly smiles for children, all working hard down in Philly to be somebody, completely ignored the violence in the midst of their row home world, beneath the massive stone church and the large cross on the roof.

But, like my fascination with mother nature down in the valley; I was obsessed with what everyone else ignored, this drunken madman just a few houses away. I would not walk up the alley where I could be seen, but up along the back doors and garages but five houses away and found the back door unlocked, turned the door handle, opened the door, and knowing the layout which was the same for every house, walked past the two iron tubs to my right, then a few yards up past the water-heater, and there I was, a seven year old boy at the bottom of a pair of stairs exactly as my own house, standing frozen in one spot, leaning over to peek up in hopes of seeing Mr. Farnsworth that I could hear so distinctly." Fucking, goddam, fucking, god dam, fucking, god dam.." and then, a split second after he would throw an empty whiskey bottle down into the basement, breaking either on the floor at the bottom of the last step or upon hitting the water heater, raining down upon a pile of glass from six? Twelve? Fifteen? Who the hell knows, whiskey bottles or glasses? His cursing, ranting, and raging voice was so loud, so violent, so frightening; and no one even called the police; only I was a witness to it, and can still not figure out why he got away with it, and no cops ever showed up. But, I guess, that was Green Valley Road in the 1950s; a man could terrify his family, but then, bullies and nuns terrified without restraint, as we saw.

Chapter 12

Green Valley Road was only a city block long beginning on St. Lawrence Road a mere few yards from the rear entrance of St Lawrence church and it's large parking lot and equal distance from the University of Pennsylvania's farm and Observatory's southwest corner fence, backed by a small forest of bushes and trees on the opposite side of the church properties.   The small two story red brick row houses were simple in design, but many of the occupants, though appearing "simple," were quite unique, especially to a young boy who got to know them somewhat while delivering the newspaper, milk, and bread seven days a week for three or four years; received as if a machine were delivering their basic needs, and not much more than a machine when the boy collected the fees, originally just quietly polite and as invisible as other forms in misty early mornings, until the boy's curiosity got the best of him after listening and learning about his customers by ease-dropping upon adult conversations after Sunday mass. Gradually, he tapped into his customers psychic with not just small talk, but complements appealing to their egos, on bill paying days.

The third house in on the south side of Green Valley Road was the Duffy family whose daughter, it was rumored, had become the object of affection of a guy who would become one of the greatest football running backs in all of Philadelphia sports history, who lived cattycorner on Academy Lane across from my family home on Green Valley Road, the main hero of my life at the time, which meant nothing to me on collection day when the Duffy only child, Barbara Duffy, who was charged with paying all the delivery men, which included my young emerging manhood. Barbara Duffy always came to the door with a big smile on her beautiful face, long blond hair, and always, always wearing a fluffy white pullover sweater, that, accentuated her large breasts, with two nipples poking out from behind, with their natural nipple shapes behind the contours of the fluffy white, as full and stiff as beneath my baggy pants, which soon became difficult to hide, and so obvious to her, that her smile began with eye to eye contact that left my legs quivering as her eyes would glace down at my bulging pants, her white smiling teeth as white as the sweater. That is when she handed me the money.

But Barbara Duffy, as sexy as the pin-ups G.I.s were pinning up on their lockers during WW II, was already spoken for, he being my first hero ever, whose home was but less than a football away, on Academy Lane that was just an extension of Green Valley Road. His name was Charlie Albertus, and he may be the very best running back athlete to ever come out of Philadelphia, and that is, of course, saying a lot with guys like Reds Colletta, Johnny Papus, Emery McCourt, Reds Bagnell to name only a few. But Charlie could do it all, for he was a gifted natural athlete who would star in any sport he chose.

I think he was my first live hero. There I was but ten years old sitting in the old basement church on Sunday morning's always sitting in the same area knowing I would get to see the Albertus family of four who always sat in the pews off to the left side at the front of the church, the side closest to Green Valley Road.

In the 1940s and 1950s Philadelphia's high school games often drew more fans than the professional Eagles, many high school games played in the same building, called Connie Mack Stadium, with high school games drawing from thirty to sixty thousand fans from different parts of this tough city with more factories, refineries, and ship building enterprises than perhaps any other city in America; and these high school players were the sons and grandsons of those who worked these tough well-paying jobs most often passed on to sons who were not supposed to think of college, but a good job at Westinghouse or Sun Oil, or GE, of dozens of other major industrial industries where you worked for decades and then retired; football players fighting for one thing, tribal rights, the kids often looking more like their older fathers and uncles than high school students, with faces etched with creases and scars mostly seen on grown men. Then did not look like, or act like, boys.

Why, I would sit in that church on Sunday mornings in awe of watching this Charlie Albertus walking up to receive communion, he looking more like a young handsome New York actor with short dark hair and the lean body more of a basketball player than a football star he was, my thinking more about all those tough, scar-faced like middle aged men, powerful, violent, guys on the field this same day, Italians in south Philly, German and Polish in north Philly, the Irish of West Catholic, and my intense thought of what Charlie was thinking having to face these tough mean looking men that looked no different to me than the hardened WW II vets playing for the Philadelphia Eagles; no wonder Nancy with nipples sticking out of her white wooly sweater was in love with him, and not her newspaper delivery boy.

But like many hero's, Charlie's image took some strange turns. After high school, Charlie married Nancy and afterward I found out where they were living in a first-floor apartment but a few feet from West Chester Pike, and but a hundred yards east of the funeral home. One night, alone, and with this new found knowledge of where they lived, I was totally surprised that I could actually look in their window and see the two of them, her in a white robe standing at an ironing board, and he; shocking my young romantic sensibilities, was actually walking around, in front of her, completely naked. That Catholic Knight I used to see standing in line waiting for communion was walking around in front of the most beautiful girl I had ever seen in my young life, with no clothes, whatsoever. A disgrace. Then I walked home in a state of utter confusion.

Then, my hero goes to the University of Pennsylvania on a football scholarship, for Penn in those days just after WW II not only played Notre Dame and other top football universities, but had winning seasons against these top schools, with returning WW II veterans from Philadelphia and Pennsylvania who were old enough and seasoned enough to play pro football at the time, such as Chuck Bederarick and others like Frank Cooney who had fought the toughest of the German army at the Battle of the Bulge. That was Penn in those days when my hero steeped onto the practice fields at Hershey Pennsylvania. Charlie, historically chosen first string with all his natural talents; but on one given day the Penn coach put Charlie's West Catholic co-star, and future Princeton all-America, the infamous "Reds Bangnell, who did not have the natural talent gifted to Charlie, on the first string backfield, the coach pissed at Charlie's attitude in summer camp. Charlie, standing on the sideline for the first time ever, looked out at this scene that was normal to many, as if in a nightmare from another person's life, he suffering a complete disconnect, simple walked off the field to the locker room, changed into his clothes, and never played another day at football. Talk about a "moment in time."

When sitting in that church adoring my football hero I never thought of his father, just him, but his father was a local champion golf player and as always, with Charlie's natural athletic talents he soon mastered golf as he had football, and with his football career ended, he perceived an opportunity to make not only some good money, but perhaps after four years with West Philly street kids he learned that a good con was worth an honest day's work, and he soon used his golf talents to make more money than any job he could sign onto in Philly.

Back in the day, there were always brash young guys as well as doctors and lawyers who used golf as a gambling venture that was widely popular but remained in the shadows of county club society; my Charlie took full advantage of these shadows. He would agree to meet a golfer on his home course betting a rather modest, mostly gentlemanly sum of money that Charlie always seemed to lose, and rather graciously; followed by the universally accepted return engagement on home turf.

Charlie, has always been one of the most sincerely charming of boys, and now as a man whom men cherished getting to know, for his high school stardom bordered on a deep Philadelphia legendary list of guys perhaps more respected than most professional Eagles players. Charlie knew this, and used it, for the somewhat startled, or just plainly confused golfers now playing on Charlie's home course for such high money stakes, way beyond the simple hundreds of dollars they anticipated betting, and now loosing tens of thousands of dollars to this guy they respected so much; ripping then off like the hustler which he had become. But his dealings with many of these pretentious, cheap, elitist bastards, tying to make a buck, and I cheered my hero, again. But he won so much money from so many that he was soon not allowed to golf on any of the high-class Philadelphia country clubs. Charlie's story gets rather murky, and all I can remember is that his wife divorced him and after years of heavy drinking, he died an alcoholic. Before any stones are thrown his way, I just wonder how much damage was done to his brain playing for West Catholic in the 1940s when helmets were nothing more than a thin leather padded head gear, with what we are learning in the 21 century about football and the human brain, so much so that many communities have banned children under a certain age from playing the sport. I like to think that the real Charlie was that mature good-looking kid standing in line on Sunday morning to receive communion, then knelt in prayer as my little astonished eyes fixated on him, wondering what prayers he was saying in preparation for that Sunday's game. Life has a way of peeling away much of what was once considered not only unique but basic aspects of our very being, leaving many with nothing much left that distinguishes them from anyone else.

Chapter 13

The adults on Green Valley Road harbored something none of us kids had any inclinations of, nor did the adult behaviors give away this thing they keep to themselves, individually and collectively, for most had pleasant personalities and smiles and laughter was common and expected of them, and they mostly all dressed nicely, or one could say, dressed for success, so many looked as if they ran a company or were bankers, which some were; but again, these adults were the products of the Great Depression of the 1930s and grew up in families struggling to put food on the table. Many of them knew suffering, and often scolded us at dinner tables for not eating what was before us, "When I was your age we were lucky to have one meal a day," and on and on at times, something young kids with refrigerators and kitchens stuffed with enough food to feed an army platoon for a week could grasp with this only reality they knew, for the parents unknowingly stocked up on sometimes excessive food supplies triggered by memories, some just beneath the surface, others deep in the subconscious, of hunger during some deadly years of the depression, with conscious memories of young parents whom they only remember as old, for economic depressions do this to people. Perhaps this is one of the reasons why Sunday mass was not just a Catholic obligation to attend less one commit a sin by not attending; but became, easy in hindsight to suggest, a way to purge one's innermost fears of living that life of constantly threatening poverty and in indignities resulting from that dreadful condition so many lived as children themselves. Put on that expensive looking three piece suit that speaks of not just money, but authority and the success that flows from being a well-dressed man or woman; the later with not just beautifully designed dresses and caps, but hats that in hindsight would be worn by women on fifth avenue in new York city rather than a Sunday mass at St. Lawrence.

But they carried it off magnificently, for none of us kids had any inkling of just how hard our parents early lives had been despite their talks about why we should eat what was before us, with gratitude, for to us they carried themselves, and dressed the part, of levels of similar success we saw in characters on the movie screens of the 1940s and '50s. Writing this in 2019 makes me think: increased global hostilities and the global proliferation of the deadliest weapons in world history could possibly wipe out nine-tenths of today's world population; but that one-tenth that remained would carry on with the same self-assured positive attitudes of my parents Great Depression generation on Green Valley Road, looking the part of success, no matter what the reality of life one has to face.

Chapter 14

But sports and athletic prowess were the core values by which everything and everyone was judged in this culture of ours, and if you had any smarts, you played it down with an unspoken acceptance, even for those who were fortunate enough to go to private high schools, it was the good athletes and tough guys who were most respected. So taking a glance up Green Valley Road scanning all the row houses it was this that consciously and sub-consciously stopped the scan momentarily; like just four or five front doors on the right hand side as one walks west up pops Al Brancato, a man who would stand by his front lawn with eyes sparkling with joy, a smile on his face, thick long arms with one always extended to reach out to shake the hands of us kids as if we were equal to the adults. When most of us kids were only three Al played third base for the Philadelphia Athletics Class-A farm system. The star short-stop, Skeeter Newsome, has suffered a fractured skull, and Brancato who had never played short-stop was called up by the manager, the famous Connie Mack, to fill in when he had never before played short-stop, for Connie Mack was enticed by what he called the 20 year old's " cannon right arm." When WW II broke out Brancato enlisted in the US Navy, but after returning to the "A.s" after the war he appeared in just ten games, then bounced around in organized baseball but never again played in the big leagues. But, on Green Valley Road Al Brancato was our hero who had played for the infamous Connie Mack, in the same house named "Connie Mack Stadium" where we high schoolers played many of our games, drawing upward of thirty to forty thousand fans just to see Philadelphia high school football in the l950s.

Just a few doors up from Mr. Broncato lived the first truly nasty bully I would encounter, a boy a few years older than all of us on Green Valley Road, named Andy Trebino, who punched and kicked nearly every kid in the extended neighborhood.   To us, Andy looked as old as our uncles, with an adult nose, a mouth curved like an angry poster image, and dark suspicious unreadable eyes that we young kids avoided, at all costs, for he would turn on you for just looking into his eyes.   Yea, a real bastard. The strange thing in my young mind, I was supposed to call this terrorist my cousin, for my father and his father not only worked together as loom-fixers in a West Philadelphia textile plant, but the father was my father's "Best Man" when he married my mother. But the kid was a son of a you know what. For some strange reason he left me alone physically, even though he used what I would years later experience and teach, psychological warfare, to keep me off balance, not just on Green Valley Road but at Pilling's Lake in Clementon New Jersey where his parents owned a summer cabin, just across the railroad tracks and down below the hill upon which my cousin Joe Lynch lived with my uncle and aunt, next to a pond with a small island in the center with a small red and white wooden three foot tall housing for the ducks, most of which we brought from Philly not long after the Easter holidays surprise gifts of cute little yellow ducks, now grown to semi-ugly smelly creatures in the basement, later resurrected as white feathered year-round wild pets who could now fly a few hundred yards to pristine fast moving hidden streams filled with native fish of all sizes only unavailable during winter with water turning to steel hard ice, a natural tranquil setting of peace on the property of the high strung Trabino family, housing Andy, who in the summer months would attempt to bully and intimidate his cousin, and my cousin, Joe Lynch living up on that hill above the railway tracks.

My blond-haired cousin Joe was redneck skinny and tough as one, and when attacked by Andy would return with fist-ti-cuffs after taking l-p bloodied punches from this nasty bully, who was known to punch other young guys in the face as they waited to climb to up the high diving board to dive into the pine dark waters of Pilling's Lake. By the time I was a sophomore in high school Andy sensed not to screw with me anymore; but seven years later after I had been discharged from the military and was a freshman in college we met again; this time at a party when Andy had his wife with him, a beautiful thin and shy blond, my feeling somewhat sorry for the young lady. It was here that I somehow got Andy into a corner of the kitchen and looked him in the eyes, with my feet planted not just squarely on the ground, but in that unspoken position only street-fighters recognize, and told him,

" Andy, I am hoping that you give me some shit tonight like you gave to all us guys on Green Valley Road back then," …uh…uh..Teddy, what are you talking about…" Shut the fuck up Andy…listen…eyes now locked into confrontation into fear: " I will kick your ass out the door, you bastard; please, just give me an excuse to break your fat nose and knock out a few of your teeth as you did to us back them.." Uh..Uh…uhh… take it easy Teddy… take it easy…" as he backed down like the bully always does, this time nearly a decade after his Green Valley Road violence.

Chapter 15

Beyond Andy's house on that north side of Green Valley Road were a series of houses with families we rarely encountered, a sort of quiet section of homes where the families quietly went about their lives nearly invisible in relation to this row-house culture with dozens of young noisy boys laughing and running often bouncing balls of all types onto their lawns and sometimes hitting their front windows, though never drawing a response on those occasions. Then came the O'Leary household of mother, father, and son, Richard, who was known as Dick O'Leary to us kids was a lean blond haired shy boy who like me had natural swimming abilities, his backstroke of such championship character he was asked to try out for the swim team our first semester in high school, difficult, because there were no freshman or JV teams, only the varsity whose roster rarely contained a freshman. My pal Dick told me that he was very nervous about this try-out and asked me to join him, O'Leary secretly believing I had sufficient talent to make the team, and low and below, we were the only freshmen they kept, but making the team was ok, but what I really wanted was to be a football player, and having just been cut as a freshman was glad to have made the swim team, still determined to make the football team during our spring semester tryouts. During swim season both Dick and I won more races than all the seniors put together and appeared destined to achieve more in the years to come.

Then during the summer months something strange was happening with O'Leary, his behavior was rapidly changing, but unbeknownst to me for I spent most of the summer months away from Philadelphia camping up in Connecticut with family and only heard about this upon returning, and by that time much damage had occurred, and this dear friend of mine was looked down upon and ridiculed by children and adults alive.

The behavior: O'Leary would sit on the crest of people's lawns in the middle of the afternoons where he would rub his hands over his pants at the crotch for long periods of time before coming in his pants, to the horror of grow-ups viewing him, eventually calling the police who first booked him, and then to the psychiatric hospital ward for observation shortly after I returned.

And, not before I did the rounds of the neighborhood seeking out the worst of the bullies that had tormented O'Leary; for even thought his behavior discussed me also, I just knew deep down inside that this was not my pal, I had no idea what it was, but I was not going to lose faith in him, and now that I was home no bullies were going to go unpunished.

Within a short time, O'Leary was admitted into the hospital for an operation, for they had discovered a large tumor in his head that turned out not to just be cancer, but so advanced my pal was dead within a week. I soon quit the swim team and never swam in high school competition again. I never forget O'Leary, especially years later when my only son died of a brain tumor as well.

Chapter 16

The house on Green Valley Road that produced the most amazing families was numbered 129. The first friend of my life, at three, lived there, the oldest of six children. Charles, who began first grade with me, quickly moving to not only the front of the class, but the seat reserved for the best student in the class, years later graduating from a five year chemical engineering degree from the prestigious Drexel University who worked one day in the field for a large Philadelphia firm before quitting, having decided to become a medical doctor proceeded to take the medical school entrance exams called the MCATS that normally qualify one for possible admittance the following year. Charlie scored one of the highest in MCAT history, thus, he was allowed to register for medical school just six weeks after taking the test, then completing medical school a year early with a reputation for being a genius at diagnosing medical problems so much that well established specialist would seek him out for opinions with diagnosing difficult cases, and this at one of the top medical schools in Philadelphia. Charlie's mother wanted him to set up private practice above the local drug store in their new neighborhood further out on the main line after moving from our row house Green Valley Road, his mother "not wanting to live in a neighborhood with "factory workers," of which there were only one, my father, but within hours of his medical school graduation Charlie was recruited by the CIA who sent him around the world for a decade analyzing the health of dangerous dictators and other clandestine missions revealed to me, his best pal, and only me, with trust I never reveal, he knowing my own military intelligence background and secrets, neither of us should have shared. He had a brother, Donald, who would become a thirty-year FBI agent, and another brother, Richard, who was a quick and brilliant guy who spent years as a stock broker, later made a fortune selling land for development in Florida.

But Charlie was the seven year old kid that would wonder through the woods and forest with me hunting at first with a bow and arrow, then a bee-bee gun, and then our .22 pump rifles, which we bought from caddy money, taking them apart to smuggle into our homes hiding them beneath our bed frames until we took them out into the vast forested areas outside suburban Philadelphia back in the 1940s; ten, eleven year old's thinking of themselves as hunters seen on old Hollywood movies of the time. Once in the woods and forest, we shot anything that moved; fortunately, we never saw another human.

But one day after spending hours without seeing any deer, rabbits, pheasants, or other prey we were bored by the time we returned to pick up our bikes we had hidden near West Chester Pike in what was known as the "Old Burdaugh Mansion," a former Main Line estate high up on a hill over-looking this main road of West Chester Pike.

The building at one time had housed one of the wealth Main-Line families from the late 19. century into the l920s and beyond, whose unique story centers around a young son who refused to serve in WW I and tried to hide out in the scattered buildings that made up the estate with strange and often conflicting stories with the authorities seeking to arrest him, followed by the demise of the family fortune after the 1929 financial collapse followed by the Great Depression.

Charlie and I loved to visit this place that was always vacant with its pedestrian view of two businesses on the Pike, "Smitty's Sawmill" whose lumber cutting saws could be heard throughout the small valley in which it was located, the aroma of freshly cut timber that we could smell from our perch behind one of the thick walls of the mansion up on high.

The other business was a truck-stop dinner across the street from the sawmill, a one-story type of joint that could be found on rural roads across America in the 1940s. One day, that both of us have talked about all our lives, in complete disbelief, without any intelligent explanation of our behavior that day Charlie and I aimed our 22 pump rifles at the roof of that dinner and began firing round after round into the roof, both of us not admitting to ourselves or to each other, that before every time we pulled the trigger, our subconscious images of 1940s WW II films and cowboy movies drove our stupid unthinking behavior that only saw the roof, only the roof, with no conscious appreciation for the fact that people were beneath that roof, until several, then more, than many people ran out of the dinner onto the street looking up in every direction for the source.

The fact that no one was hit, wounded, or killed was a miracle. It was only when we saw the large number of people standing outside near the Pike, did we realize what a stupid thing we had done. The smiles evaporated from our faces, we said nothing to each other, disassembled our 22 rifles, stashed them in our bags, grabbed our bikes, walked them down the dirt path to the pike, and innocently rode past the dinner with the dozen or so people still outside looking around in disbelief not taking any notice of the two young boys riding east on their bikes. It was something Charlie and I never discussed for a long time, until years later when Charlie as an M.D., and me as a Ph.D. was discussing how young people around the world were involved in violent crime and wars in their societies.

The second family to live at 129 Green Valley Road had three boys and the oldest a sister; six people living in that small row house, the father a banker from and now working in South Philly who every day took the local trolley car to 69. Street, then the elevated train to 15ths street in Philly, and then a bus down broad street to the bank.

His oldest son Billy became my new best friend who happened to be a very fast runner at a time when I had begun running long distances in the summer of my high school freshman year while camping with my family near the ocean in Connecticut where I would leave the beach and run the four miles to Niantic and back again, nearly a ten mile run. In the summer of l951 no one ran on roads but boxers and those who ran track, and to see a young guy running on a highway was just not done, in fact, many laughed and considered me "nuts," particularly when they noticed I ran barefooted all the way.

By the time we had returned to Philly for the new school year I had lost about thirty pounds of fat and with the weight training had replaced much of the weight with muscle. In the evenings Billy and I would meet up and just begin running, anywhere, and everywhere; just running and running, sometimes all the way out to the Philadelphia airport and back to Green Valley Road. And, by the way, we did wear running shoes.

By the time Billy was a senior at West Catholic high school he won the Pennsylvania state track championships in both the 100 yard-dash and the 220 yard-dash; making him the fastest track star in all of Pennsylvania.

Billy served in the USAF for four years, married, had three beautiful daughters, and became a very successful insurance man running offices in New York City and then Boston with his wife as his main assistant, in both places hiring their own staff of over a hundred employees who all worked so well together that profits soared for Prudential; but, then something sinister happened. Prudential screwed him by closing the office and moving him to an office in Rochester New York; where he again build up a good business for Prudential, and again bought a home for his wife and three daughters.

Now with a large beautiful home for his family with all the expenses associated with this lifestyle including private schools and the rest with his wife now retired to take care of the homestead and having nothing to do with the insurance business.

The company that had encouraged the move from the extremely successful and very well-run organization in Boston to up-state New York, screwed Billy to the wall by firing him. He was mortified, but kept the family in the dark that he was now without a job. Every morning Billy would go through his normal routine; coffee and reading the newspaper, kissing his three daughters before their leaving for school, dressing in one of his three-piece suits and kissing his wife goodbye, then driving away as if going to the office.

Only Billy knew the reality. His love for his family was at the heart of his character. His love for his wife had grown and grown as he was more and more attracted to her as the years went by, and he just adored his daughters who excelled as students in school and were the most popular within whatever environment they were active; school, sports, social events, church settings, you name it. Billy's daughters, Billy's wife, were what Billy lived for, worked for, the basis of his very existence. For them, he would take a bullet to his heart.

Day after day, week after week, month after month Billy interviewed with dozens and dozens of insurance companies and financial institutions in search of a well-paying position to support not just his life-style, but his family. Reader, tell me, what the hell is it about our culture that somehow turns against those who have worked their way up to a respectful position in life, and when facing a dirty turn of events, are not just ignored, but more or less shunned into a consciousness of isolation, as if they were condemned to failure. Billy could not believe all the negative responses and reactions to his applications, a man who had been so successful in the tough markets of Manhattan and Boston, and on one interview was shocked with facing a guy he had not only hired years ago in Manhattan but advanced him within Prudential Insurance to the extent that a corporate raider hired the guy at just the time Billy was negotiating a huge contract the guy had worked on, leaving Billy exposed, and losing millions. Now this same guy sat facing Billy as if they were meeting for the first time, and left the room as one of his secretaries announced he had an important phone call to deal with, never returning, with a secretary handing Billy a business
card, "sorry, we have no openings at this time, but call us next month, Mr. so and so, regrets he has no openings at this time. Billy walked out of that interview with his head spinning, his heart pumping, his Irish spirit enraged beyond comprehension. It felt as if the world itself had turned against him. How was he going to support, protect, and pay for all that made his family secure and happy? He had not told his wife but all their huge savings were nearly gone, and with no job, no income, what the hell was he to do.

Billy had not only been a Pennsylvania state running champion, but was a champion wide receiver in not only pick-up games but on semi-pro tough Philadelphia teams where few defensive backs could hardly defend against not only his flash-fast moves but his gifted hands that did not drop footballs. This was his essence, long before business success.

After this interview he drove around Rochester in a daze, thinking about how, unknown to his family, he had only recently begun to get notices of foreclosure and utility shut-offs as well as threats to the four vehicles the family drove. When he went into a convenience store to buy a beer to calm his nerves he also bought a toy gun that a young kid was looking at as his mother was pulling him away. Why? He had no conscious idea. None. He just bought it.

Passing bank after bank: Citibank, Home Federal Savings, Rochester Savings Bank, Securities Trust Company: bingo, "fuck it, he said to himself, parked his car about ten blocks away, walked back to Citibank, walked into the bank, of course looking as if he belonged with his dapper silk tie and three piece suit, and at this late hour he was surprisingly the only customer. The young lady behind the counter smiled and said, "what can I help you with?' and a split second later, Billy, put one hand on the counter, and a second later, vaulted over the counter, his feet hitting the floor as the young lady froze in fear as he exposed the toy gun.

" GIVE ME ALL THE MONEY YOU HAVE, AND DO NOT ACTIVATE THE ALARM SYSTEM," his hand as steady as if he had been robbing banks all his life, and the young lady shaking as if she were going to faint as she put thousands of dollars in bills into a bank bag, her hand shaking, handing it to Billy, who in a split second put his hand onto the counter and vaulted over it, and within a flash was out the door sprinting down side streets like the champion runner he was reaching his parked car with the bag of money and driving off, then across town to his family bank where he deposited enough cash to cover the entire month's expenses that had hours before threatened to disclose the new reality.

Billy, soon known in news reports as "The Leaper," robbed Securities Trust Company three times, Rochester Savings once, Citibank once, Home Federal Savings once, for a total amount of $65,000 from October 1977 until February 1981, until he was caught.

When I asked Billy about that he told me that deep-down inside he wanted to be caught for on that last "job" he did something he had never done before. Always Parking his car at least ten blocks away... remember....he could run; and always attaching a stolen or phony license plate to his car, this one time he just kept his legally authorized New York State plate, which did him in.

After robbing a bank and running the ten blocks back to his car someone casually saw him and thought he looked very suspicious and took down his license plate number and called 911 to report a suspicious character, and the description matched Billy's profile. Within an hour, the police were at his home and he was arrested, later tried, and after a great deal of legal dealings and support from hundreds of people attesting to Billy's outstanding character and corporate screwing; he received a sentence of only four years in prison, which he carried out with dignity, before being released. "The Leaper", my life-long pal and brother whom I will always love and respect, was free again.

Chapter 17

But during those years of the late 1940s and early 1950s subtle changes were taking place in the minds of the young, for while they gave respect and deference to parents and their culture of conservative values first transmitted from recently and not so recent immigrant families glad to have roots in America and a shot at the American dream of steady work, a roof over one's head, and food on the table, we were more or less the third generation out, beyond this ritualized deference there was this powerful, exciting, bold, revolutionary, challenge to all our parents had tried to instill in our minds; it was called "Rock and Roll," and did we rock, and one song said it all, "rock around the clock."

We were the rock and roll generation, and we left our families sitting before the new mind conforming technology called TV, we were out there dancing are asses off as if the world was about to end tomorrow. It began slowly with the likes of Bill Haley and the Comets but soon we had the true revolutionary wild men such as Jerry Lee Lewis and Little Richard who blew the lid off all the pretentions that guided our parents cultural norms, exposing the animal and irrational passions our parent's culture tried to protect us from.

Jerry Lee Lewis and Little Richard did for our psychic than what the storming of the Bastille did for the French Revolution, or what the February and October revolutions did for Lenin's revolution, or the Boston Tea Party did for the American Revolution. There would be no return.

Our parents rejoiced with buying a new automobile to drive around the city; we bought very old pre-WW II huge four door monsters for often less than a hundred dollars, and with gasoline prices as cheap as a hamburger, drove them across country to California or down into the unpopulated barrens of Florida, feeling a freedom on the open road our parents never dreamed about. We felt free, and even though we had little or no money, we moved around the country in ways that even today astonishes me, for today, without DeNiro, you can't get very far-o.

Up on Green Valley Road we may have been just a mile above the streets of West Philly below, but the cultural divide during these times was as if we were fifty miles apart; for all those liberating things were held somewhat under acceptable control, but down into West Philly a pulsating magnetic energy flashed with hypnotic powers from neighborhood to neighborhood down into South Philly and up into North Philly, with men singing on street corners, dancing in clubs with young ladies before live bands, influencing young people nation-wide through the "Bandstand" TV show at 46. and Market Street in West Philadelphia, a few blocks from our West Catholic high school. What had begun with the local Bill Haley and the Comets exploded beyond them with Elvis, Jerry Lee Lewis, Little Richard, Fats Domino and others, thus the early 1950s gave birth to the "Rock & Roll" generation, a revolution in culture whose existence pre-dates a later cultural   revolution in the 1960s.

Like other generations before us, we thought it would never end. That this new rock and roll music would not just play over and over and over for years and years, but it was an end in itself, part of not just our existence, but the existence of the next generation, and the next, and the next; for nothing could top the rock and roll that drove our parent's generation crazy and convinced us we were special and proof of which was that right here in Philly where it all began with Bill Haley (actually his first gig was in Gloucester City N.J. across the Delaware River from Philly). we had a national television program where gals and guys, many of whom we actually knew, danced to the music with their young faces and gyrating bodies viewed by eyes in every town of the United States that had television reception, "Bandstand" was hot.

"hot," yes, but I must confess that many Philly tough guys, including myself, liked to see the girls dancing, but the men, we often considered, somewhat "sissy," until some of our tribe who were local boxers who jumped rope, could not avoid the rythmatic vibrations picked up by their bodies and became some of the best dancers.

My dancing? Did not begin till stationed overseas on military bases where I would gather on a Saturday night with other members of our boxing team, and me being the only white guy received an education in rhythm and dance. My black brothers would create music out of nothing; tapping on the unturned bottoms of trash cans, slapping their hands against their thighs, tapping on the stone floor with medal and wooden objects, and singing as if accompanied by a full band: they were just great.

As we all sat in a circle, one guy would get up into the center and do an impromptu dance, all by himself, as if in a trance with a huge smile on his face, in rhythm with the sounds now bouncing off the four walls and ceiling as if we were in a sound studio. All being boxes who jumped rope, so their movements were nothing short of spectacular.

Then one night, they all pointed to me, and yelled, "Get off your fat white ass and dance," prompted by my best pal on the team and on the base, and my room-mate, Jim Jenkins from Newark who boxed, jumped rope, and not only mimicked the great boxer, the original Sugar Ray Robinson, but was as handsome as him and built like him. With Jim physically nearly pushing me off my seat, I was up in the center of all my brothers for the first time, and it all began. I solo danced, and never stopped.

After my four years of military I arrived to college in 1958 at a time when white college kids had not yet got into the full swing of it, I took the young ladies onto the dance floor and moved like white men did not, at the time, and never stopped dancing, was in the moment when the 60s hit. I owed it all to my black brothers from the military boxing teams.

And on Green Valley Road, no one could come close to dancing like that.

Chapter 18

But, still what remained at the forefront of my mind, was football, specially the football played at West Catholic, officially known as "West Philadelphia Catholic High School for Boys, and nine out of ten kids within its urban and suburban jurisdiction would give up anything to be able to play for West Catholic, whose mythic images and championship stories we all grew up with, as today's youth do with professional teams. Back in the day Eagles stars were less revered than kids from North Catholic, Northeast Public, Southern, Roman and other Philadelphia teams that played with such passion, one could argue was similar to the U.S. Marine Corp motivation of due or die.

So, if you came to West Catholic to play football you had to be tough, first off the field, and then on the field if you were lucky enough to make the team. To this day I still vividly remember my first day as a freshman, one of perhaps over a thousand students, for when we graduated four years later our class was nine hundred, so perhaps that freshman class was larger.

On that first day I accidently met a guy who would become the best friend of my entire life. Each lunch period was filled with so many in a cafeteria whose physical environment resembled more of a prison than a school, to feed over three thousand students in shifts of hundreds, given fifteen minutes to consume the food, then forced out onto the athletic field where it was mandatory to walk around the quarter mile track for a half hour before the next class session.

The hundred yard-long football field with goal posts at either end was surrounded by this quarter mile cinder track, both lying but twenty five yards or so from the elevated sub-way cars that ran overhead from 69 street to downtown and back; whose existence was somehow minimalized in our minds, equating the trains as if they were people in the stands watching our so very important existence.

On this first day of classes, the field, that had during the summer grown thick with green grass was somewhat dotted with grass-less brown dirt patches form the late August summer football practices, as we walked the track. We were not allowed to stop for any reason or step onto the field, with one or more Christian Brothers making sure we did not, with 300 or more boys walking around the track, some trying desperately to pass smoking forbidden cigarettes from one hand to the other while waving hands to blow away the smoke from the eyes of the Brothers, watching, watching, watching.

And then, on this first day, it happened. A verbal argument broke out between two freshmen that led to fists being thrown rather quickly, immediately surrounded by a very thick circle of onlookers, for we liked nothing more than a good fight, and there I was right in the middle of the onlooking crowd of shouting, laughing, yelling freshmen as the two pugilist throwing bare-fisted knuckles, already drawing blood.

The monitoring Brothers who would have come down hard on any cigarette smokers detected by them, more or less laid back from student fist-fights unless they lasted too long, or attached too large a crowd of onlookers, so they did nothing to break up the fight.

I personally really enjoyed watching, but was somewhat taken back by a guy directly across from me who seemed to enjoy it more than I. His large very bright blue eyes shone like none of the others with a white toothed grin etched in a smiling Irish face that stood out like a beacon above the shouts and laughter, and when one of the fighters was knocked to the ground by a blow to the jaw heard all the way up to the elevated train platform, a Brother finally came in to break up the crowd of students, but not before this guy caught me looking his way as we somehow just walked over, shook hands, and introduced ourselves. "I'm Jim Boyle," he said as we shook hands, neither of us knowing that we would be live-long pals.

We ending up playing right next to each other for three years on the football team, he a center and me a pulling guard, upon graduation we both turned down football scholarships, not wanting to study but to see the world, decided to join the Marines until Jim's mother objected, then to be Army paratroopers, again she objected saying, "fighting is all you guys do now; join the Air Force and learn something besides fighting." Jim's Mom was a widow raising nine children on her own, herself with Irish Sullivan blood. Jim and his brothers always obeyed Mom, and since he was my best pal, I also joined the Air Force, while my heart was a Marine or a paratrooper. To our displeasure, the tests we were forced to take, sent us to military intelligence schools for a year, and then out on duty where we learned more than we bargained for with our top-secret clearances, our experiences a book all to itself. After the military we became competitive surf boat rowers representing North Wildwood beach patrol, and when I married Jim was my best man, and my best all-around pal not from Green Valley Road.

But the motivation at the very center of football was respect, and the most respected at our 3000 all male student body, was who was toughest, and they were not the hero runners and passers, but the linemen. Mostly Irish or Italian guys who could knock you over in a second or even knock you out. Most were big guys, but I, but five feet nine, not only made the team but after banging heads in what we called "blood pits." It was tense for us Younger freshman, where larger upper-classmen, who looked as old as our uncles to us, were so much stronger and hit so much harder and faster. We wore no face masks in those days that protect the nose and teeth, and it was really frightening to look up and see a face resembling a grown man whose eyes were flashing with fury as if he wanted to kill you with a forearm smash that often broke noses or knocked out some of our teeth.

There were no holes-barred in the blood pit; but those older guys were gentleman at heart, and did not intentionally wish to hurt any of us freshman, they just wanted us to learn what they knew of line-play, so we would be able to step into their shoes, so to speak, as some of his did the following year. But perhaps, more immediately important, they wanted us to try and be tough enough to prepare them to go against the strong Philadelphia Catholic league teams we would face; such as North Catholic with big tough guys of Polish and German extraction, or South Catholic with huge Italian guys whose dark facial whiskers had us feeling as if we were playing against men our uncles ages. Many of the kids of the 1950s, sure did not look like "kids."

When you walked the streets of Philadelphia in the 1950s with a West Catholic letter sweater you gained instant respect, for with twenty to forty thousand people attending high school games, you were somebody, more than kids that aspired to be doctors or lawyers, reflective of what a tough town Philly was, and still is. Of course, the kids going to school out on the Main-Line as it was called, where more into such professional ambitions, but we considered them "sissies," these kids who would eventually attend the Ivy League University of Pennsylvania; but even here we had our own perception of Penn. After WW II Penn's football team was awesome, powerful with many WW II veterans who had fought in such as the Battle of the Bulge and Imo Jima, and beat teams such as Notre Dame, Army, and Navy. Our line coach, Frank OCooney was one of them, who would bring the legendary Eagle Chuck Bederarick, with whom he played with at Penn, to our practices, and when we played in the City Championship game it was at the University of Pennsylvania Franklin Field, the same stadium where the Eagles not only played, but beat legendary Vince Lombardy's Green Bay Packers for the 1960 championship.

So, in the early 1950s when I walked Green Valley Road with that blue and white West Catholic sweater with the football letter at my hip, the only guy to do so since Charlie Albertus in the late 1940s, I was somebody.

Chapter 19

As a young boy all adults were considered threatening till proven otherwise, and those who showed any signs of acceptance and kindness, at bottom line not calling our parents telling then about our transgressions. It seemed, when they were talking with you, they were trying to find out what it was that was wrong with you. Georgie Walsh, my altar-boy guru would say: "fuck em," but I was not that brave most of the time, for he always said if they don't treat you respectfully, just "write them off, ignore them."

But some were difficult to ignore. Next door to us lived the Green family; the father a postal service mailman and a nice guy who smoked a lot of cigs and read dozens of paperback books, who often stood in the back alley with a cig and taking a break from his crowded little house who found my tense relationship with my father humorous for he could hear my old man screaming at me through our shared row-house wall, his wife, Mrs. Green was a very frail and sweet lady, their son a nice kid, then there was Mrs. Green's mother, Mrs. Murphy and her grown son Danny, all living in that small three bedroom house at the end of Green Valley Road. Danny had been a high school basketball player and his mother was a widow; but that is only the beginning.

Mrs. Murphy, had a large German Sherard dog, a nasty dog that sat right next to her as she sat in the rap around Bay window of the row house attached to our western wall; the window facing our front door but a few feet away as she witnessed the coming and goings of not just our family but anyone who came to our front door, her eyes appearing to bulge behind her thick glasses set in a face as stoic as the stone statues lining some of the downtown Philadelphia parks, recording everything, and a few times a week would approach my mother while she was outside hanging clothes on the line or emptying trash and actually ask my mother why I came home "past mid-night on Friday night and not till three am on Saturday night," and so on and so on.

But the "so on so on" changed drastically one night, or perhaps it should be said, "horribly." I was about 16 at the time and one of my pals had a 19 year old sister who would drive us around town and somehow took a liking to me even to the extent of leaving her brother in the car and at first just walking me to my front door to say good-night, until it became a hot kissing session, with me peeking over her shoulder to make sure Mrs. Murphy was not at her post, until one night she was, and when I discretely let the young lady know, she turned her head and gave Mrs. Murphy the finger, not once, but three times as the both of us burst out laughing, before she began to walk back to her car.

Somehow, and I still can't figure out how, old, fat, crippled Mrs. Murphy who walked with a cane and whom I never saw outside the house was standing on the corner of the house holding a leach attached to the dog now not only growling and showing teeth, but what I would say were his fangs; and somewhere in the split second of an eternal moment she let go of the leach as the dog bounded across the mere twelve yard space separating it from the young lady now nearly reaching the parked car.

Somehow, instinctively, I let out a sound that fortunately reached her ears just in time, for she was able to raise her arm just as the dog leap upon her, with his teeth missing her neck but chopping down on her left forearm a split second before my third or fourth lunge, my right shoulder hitting the dogs body with the force and pop of a line-backer knocking the dog off her and onto the pavement with such force the dog was temporarily stunned, before it's claws grabbed onto my arm as its teeth went for the side of my throat.

The next few seconds are buried in the eternal memory of violence, similar to what I experience in military combat; but some way I had gotten my hands around the dog's throat as its claws ripped at my arms before I was able to chock it to death, the girl a few feet away lying in the grass crying like a baby.

Mrs. Murphy was nowhere to be seen, my friend and his sister slowly drove away, Mrs. Murphy's son Danny somehow came out and removed the dead dog from our sidewalk, I went into my house, then the medicine cabinet, cleaned the scratch wounds, and wore long sleeve shirts until they healed.

Chapter 20

We were always hungry. Our parents put good food on our tables, but we remained hungry. My pal from the second family to live at 129, the Malloy's, and I were so bored at night that we would run unbelievable distances on the streets and highways, at least for that time, such as leaving Green Valley Road and running all the way to the Philadelphia airport and back.

Bill Malloy of the Malloy family, whom I wrote had won Pennsylvania state track championships. my running with him for years increased my speed considerable. But back to the hunger.

As we ran past restaurants that neither of us nor our parents ever went nor possibly could afford, we would look at each other whenever the aroma of finely cook food caught our nostrils time and time again until one night we decided to play Robin Hood; take from the rich and give to the poor. We selected an upscale Seafood restaurant from whose kitchen's doors we had a difficult time running past, for our stomachs nearly over-whelmed our legs abilities to move, no less run.

When we peeked through the kitchen door we could see a large heavy cook working feverishly over his multiple flat frying surfaces, and off to the side where trays and trays of huge breaded shrimp stuffed with so much crab meat our mouths watered at just the sight, and as if by reflex I opened the screen door as Billy dashed in as if he were in a track meet and within a few flicks of seconds he was standing beside the cook with his hands on either side of a huge tray as the cook's head sort of shook, glancing to his right, his lazy looking eyes now enlarged, blinking as if to clear them, as a look of incredulous disbelief froze his facial expression, his arms and body more or less frozen in place as he watched Billy running toward the open screen door that I held open, the boy with the large tray disappearing from his eyesight as the door slammed shut.

It was not necessary to run too far from the back of the restaurant for no one gave chase with the cook in semi-shock and confusion mumbling to the manager, who just kept shaking his head and mumbling "what...who... what...who??"

Five blocks away we ate so much of those mouth-watering treats that we could no longer run and had to walk up the steep hill from 69 street to my home where we brought the still large quantity of these exquisite seafood treats hoping to put them in my families Frig, until my mother went into a semi-rage of questions about where we go them, not believing that someone gave them to us, as my father, with fork in hand was devouring them as if it were his last meal as my mother pleaded with him to further question Billy and I. He was too busy eating to take the time to ask us any questions.

This exploit Billy and I repeated many times, for there were quite a few up-scale restaurants along our running route throughout the city beneath Upper Darby, and we never again brought any of our sophisticated haul home. But we were never hungry again.

Chapter 21

We never had any money. But as I wrote earlier, we could make some money as a caddy at the many golf courses and Country Clubs outside of Philadelphia. After the Halfpenny family left the row house culture of 129 Green Valley Road for greener pastures in the more sophisticated Havertown we kids concentrated on caddying at Lower Merion Country Club, an internationally respected joint with more lawyers and doctors than any other club, us hoping this could translate into dollars and cents, for while there was no financial flexibility with this trade of Caddy for we received two dollars and fifty cents for each bag we carried, never any more than that set fee. The hope was that these doctors and lawyers whose extremely heavy bags with expensive iron and wooden club plus all sorts of extra shit adding to the weight would, at the end, bring us a tip. Especially, those of us who were fortunate enough to caddy for teaching pros that educated us to the more subtle aspects of golf, in addition to those of us who, like myself, spent hours and hours at a course practicing with different clubs, me fortunate to have a course right next to my home, after scaling a high barbed wire fence.

With this knowledge and experience we could help those awkward unathletic rich guys by telling them which clubs to use on the course, it was called "clubbing" them around, after watching their clumsy, awkward bodies we could suggest which club to use from a particular distance. For example, if I were to have to hit a ball some known distance, I might use a seven iron; but for this fat lawyer, I would suggest a three iron.

Enough background: So here I was, as a 17 year old caddy, with bulging arm and leg muscles, and the ability to "club" these helpless golfers around the course: I needed two bags to made a decent day's wage, which at bottom line would be five bucks for eighteen holes, and hopefully a tip.

But, the Caddy Master, a drunk name Kibbey, had a thing for me and on this day assigned me not only a single bag, but a white cloth bag that could be used by some amateur in a third world country, with just a few clubs, and the owner of the bag looked like a looser. As we all, golfers and caddies, stood on the tee of the first hole at this distinguished Lower Merion Country Club, I lost it.

When my emaciated ill clad guy was standing about ten yards away from me looking down the fairway I yelled, "HEY ASSHOLE," And threw his bag of clubs at his feet, "Stick these up your sorry Ass," I yelled, as I walked back to the Caddy shack and by the time I go to the stairs on my way out, Kibby, the Caddy master was coming up screaming at me, until I picked up the large plastic trash can and threw it down the stairs at him, knocking him to the floor before I was out the door.

My two pals, Charlie and Ed close behind me laughing their asses off as we jumped into charlie's 1939 four door limousine and speed away, them thinking that was the end of it, until I began talking about "leucite," which only Charlie understood, and responded to my plea by driving to the local Pep Boys store to buy a container of the stuff before driving back to the country club. I was not done with my revenge for depriving me of making a decent wage for the day.

Charlie could always read my mind as he did this day, and after a few moments of communication he did exactly what we both had in mind. Charlie poured the contents of the leucite into his gas tank, backed up his old car to the rear door of the three story country club building now open, and put his foot to the pedal as thick, thick, gray toxic smoke began to pour into the basement, for this shit was used to clean out auto and truck engines back in the day.

Within a short time the ugly toxic gray smoke began to pour out of the open summer windows of the first floor, and then the next two floors as tuxedo clad men and women in fine dresses became part of the smoke as they hung their heads and bodies out the upper windows, chocking and spitting in an effort to catch some fresh air; for this was a large wedding party celebrating at the country Club.

Within a few minutes we backed out and sped out the drive to the exit as police cars passed us with lights ablaze and sirens screaming.   If only I had been given two bags to carry that day.

Chapter 22

We had to find another course on which to caddy and make a few bucks and we decided upon Rolling Green Country Club that was actually closer to some of our homes located on City Line Avenue in Drexel Hill, particularly for three member of the Boyle family from Clifton Heights; Jim and his two younger brothers Richard and John, all of us in good physical shape able to carry two bags plus, and with the going rate at $2.50 per bag, we could make a decent days wage, especially if we carried two rounds from early in the morning till before sun-down, and during our first week we all made pretty dam good money.

But then, as we used to say, "the shit hit the fan," for the management put up a sign that caddy fees were being reduced from $2.50 to $2.00 per bag, and "since too many caddies were not giving enough personal attention to the golfer's, a caddy could no longer carry two bags, just one." The reasoning being that carrying one bag would allow the caddy to give his undivided attention to one golfer.

Nowhere in the entire Delaware Valley was the price per bag lower than two fifty and the most political among us, Jim Boyle, immediately gathered together all the catties to devise a strategy for how to deal with this economic injustice, and before he could finish half of the guys just got up and walked away, dejected, but not willing to fight for any rights Jim was talking about, mainly a fair wage for a good day's work.

What really got our passions up was after a small delegation led by Jim and I approached a half dozen club members going into the golf locker room asking for their help, or at least their opinion in our attempting to resolve this injustice. But, the reality: us deprived of carrying two bags, but, their saving 50 cents a day on labor left a blind spot to any empathy for our cause.

As the young caddies began to walk off cursing and swearing never to come back to Rolling Green Jim and myself yelled for all the exiting caddies to stop for a minute as we made a pitch for a strike.

"A fucking strike?" what the hell do you mean? One guy nearly as big as Jim's brother John yelled as he stopped in his tracks before turning around facing the two of us.

"Follow me," I said, as I walked down the winding tree covered entrance road to the club, soon followed by nearly twenty young guys, all pissed off.

"If this is a strike, why the hell are we walking away?" one guy yelled.

"We block any members from driving up to the club," Jim yelled back, and in a few moments, we had all walked over two hundred yards down the drive-way as members were passing us and driving up to the club-house.

"We don't let them drive up," I yelled, now stopping, the sight of a huge fallen tree by the side of the road commissioned to be cut up and carted off by the ground-keepers, a job not yet carried out.

"Let's drag this fucking tree across the road, then none of these fuckers who don't care about us can get up to the club-house."

That... huge motherfucker, one guy yelled, before I countered, "Come on, you pussies, we got here two of the biggest strongmen in all Delaware County," pointing with a huge smile at Jim's brother John and the other guy nearly as big, and within seconds over a dozen guys joined the two of them as our laughter filled the valley as what appeared to be an impossible feat, happened. Up came the huge monster of a tree and across the road it lay.
The strike had begun.

When the first members cars reached the blockade, it was Jim who greeted them with a polite, diplomatic, explanation of the strike for "Worker's rights," as he called it. Most just turned their cars around and left, a few cursed us, and within an hour the police arrived, not local cops, but Pennsylvania State Police.

To make a longer story short, the cops were pretty dam nice to us, and we obeyed their command to carry the tree back to the side of the road, and then even drove up to the club-house to talk to the people in charge in attempting to resolve our problems, returning to tell us we had no recourse but to accept their terms or leave the property, which we did, but not before organizing a meeting that night at Jim's house on Walnut Street in Clifton Heights, " to talk about what?" several pissed-off guys said, and only a dozen of the caddy's showed up for the meeting, most likely due to the cases of beer promised.

The first question at the meeting: "What the hell are we here for? Nothing we can do about it."

"Yes, there is," Jim said. "Get us some justice."

"Fuck justice, I want money for my work," another said.

"We can't do anything about that now, but we can make the bastards pay in another way."

"What the fuck you talking about?"

Jim's bright blue eyes were aglow.

"Listen up. All you guys may not know it, but two of our guys who walked out a while ago, not only walked because they were desperate for that extra few buck we should get..

"Fuckin bastards should have stayed with us, especially...

"No, no, Jim interrupted. You don't know the heart of it, both these guys lost their fathers in the last year, one got killed on the docks in Chester and the other at a South Philly warehouse accident...

Now all eyes were on Jim and all their heads were shaking up and down as if in recognition.

"My mother, and her friends bring them food when they can, and I have gone with her to both their houses; they sold most of their furniture just to eat and pay for coal to heat their homes."

"No shit," two guys said at the same time.

"So Billy and Sonny, had to go to another course to make some money to help their widowed Moms, we can't blame them for not sticking with us."

"What the hell can we do? Not a fuckin thing, we ain't got no Money to help them. My old man kicks my ass if I don't bring home a few bucks, even though he drinks it up most of the time, the bastard."

"Ok, enough Jake, let's concentrate on these two families. I got an idea."

"Go ahead."

"You see all that expensive furniture in the Club House?"

"Yea, so what, what the fuck do we care about that shit?"

"They took away Billy and Sonny's money. We take the furniture and furnish their Moms homes with them."

"You fucking crazy, how we do that?"

"Late Sunday nights, the bastards are too cheap to pay the security guards after eleven; we bring all the trucks we can get our hands on and, bingo...we clean the fucking place out."

The laughter was so loud the birds in the surrounding trees were screeching and flying about as if a bomb had gone off.

"How many are in, Jim yelled at the top of his lungs."

"A dozen roared we are all in, you crazy bastard."

At five minutes before mid-night Sunday six pick-up trucks wound their way up the hill to the main entrance of the Country Club with no running lights and no radios on, parked at the foot of the steps, and as quiet as church mice the sneaker clad guys were up the steps beneath the dim yellow security light above the large unlocked screen door entrance as all twelve passed the thick wooden door now sequestered against the wall as if to welcome them all in.

A few small lamps here and there illuminated the outlines of all four of the rooms housing expensive and sophisticated couches, tables, soft lounging chairs, large and small tables, lamps of every imaginable size, shapes, and colors, and beautiful oriental rugs of all sizes on the floor of all four rooms.

The building was as quiet as if they were on one of the fairways in the middle of the golf course, with no one to be seen or heard. It took the dozen guys about twenty minutes to move out just about everything in all four rooms. now packed into the trucks, and as quietly as they came, they left, following each other down the winding road with the light of the moon allowing them to drive without headlights.

Within just an hour and a half, as planned and worked out with Billy and Sonny who had made sure both their Moms were in bed for the night, the furniture was quietly brought into both homes and arranged as if a set designer was on board, with the bare old wooden floors of both homes now graced with thousands of dollars of magnificent oriental rugs.

Over drinks afterward in an Irish pub not far from Green Valley Road, Jim, after having a difficult time quieting down the laughing and banging of celebratory beer bottles, explained that what they did was "blessed." Causing an eruption of laughter that took a long time to end.

"Seriously guys, Catholic sacred scriptures call it "occult compensation." When a grave financial injustice is committed by one party, the party hurt by the injustice, has the right to compensate itself at the expense of the transgressor," as Jim's Irish grin widen exposing every tooth in his head as the big guy poured a full bottle of beer over his head, bringing such laughter that even the bartender yelled , "Hey you fucking crazy bastards, dim it down a few notches."

Chapter 23

Jobs, jobs, jobs ... where the words I constantly heard from my parents as did those of my new pals down in West Philly where putting food on the table was considered the number one virtue, but on Green Valley Road the emphasis was mainly on education with parents never revealing to their children, they were from the same cloth as the West Philly parents; for, we were in the "suburbs," where men wore shirts and ties.

One Christmas season when I was a very young overweight kid I got a job on what was called "69. Street," which physically began at the bottom of Market street before it became West Chester Pike that I pointed out ran a mile up a hill to Upper Darby before running twenty miles out to West Chester Pennsylvania.

"69." Street was in the 1940s and 50s what a major shopping mall in the middle of a prosperous city in America today would be like: everyone shopped on 69. street, and shoppers came from wealthy Main Line neighborhoods to poor row house West Philly to shop, eat, walk, laugh, spend, and just feel free walking up and down it's somewhat steep incline with any type of shop one could imagine at the time, and less not forget the most famous location on 69. street, who hosted more great musical shows and entertainers than could be listed in multiple pages here, TOWER THEATER, yeah, "the" Tower Theater.

Up the block on the opposite side of 69 street was a store selling Men's clothing who hired me, out a desperation during a busy Christmas season, to sell one of their specialties: "Men's Hats." The manger was a very intense man of about forty with skin so white it must have never seen the summer sun, short black greasy hair combed back on his pointy head, teeth yellowed by too much tobacco, and a nervous twitch that seemed to alternate with a smile that was about as dishonest as his handshake.

On my very first day I was taken down to the basement to survey the supply of the dress hats I was to sell, not by the manager, but another guy who was the "stock boy," who was not very friendly but after pointing out the dozens of boxes containing the hats said; " Good luck on selling these duds," and left before I could ask him what he meant, but after inspecting box after box I learned what he was referring to. The men's department hats were all so small, that none would fit even a man with the head of a child.

Then in came the women and girls with their husbands and boyfriends to try on one of the hats they had seen in the window with the light shining upon them beneath a photo of a well-dressed dude, smiling with a confidence of self-satisfaction, wearing one of our hats.

In my first week I sold over two hundred hats, to the surprise but satisfaction of both the manager and the stock boy who said he never saw such sales production of the hats. But, after all, it was Christmas and the spirits rang high all over 69 street with jingle bells and singing groups of carolers and the bells of Salvation Army echoing up and down the quarter mile famous street.

But then came the week of the new year, when the street was deserted of shoppers, but filled with those returning purchases and gifts. There was no music, no joy in the air as merchants laid off salesperson after salesperson.

But, not me. For the manager had promised my job would be good till the summer lull, and I could work part time after school hours for as long as I wished.

Then the hats came back. Every day, from the time we opened till the time we closed, nearly three-quarters of all the hats I sold. The customers main complaint: the hats shrunk up so small that only their small children could wear them. I fainted ignorance, the manager fainted denial.

What I had done, unbeknownst to the manager or the stock boy: when a customer showed interest in a particular hat of a particular color, I would go down to the stock room, grab a hat of that color, take it over to the heat vent, stick my foot in it and pull with all my might to stretch not just the inside band but the entire hat, for the heat allowed me to do so without applying so much pressure, using my foot.

With the hat still warm by the time I brought it up to the customer now looking as his reflection in the mirror, next to which was the same photo that was on the outside window with a dude wearing the same hat, it was a sale.

The problem: after taking it out of the hat box on Christmas day, the cold had reduced its size back to its normal child size hat. Thus, the end of my retail clothing store career.   And the store no longer sold hats on 69 Street.

Chapter 24

The lesson from this sales experience was: get a real job, a man's job, not a sissy's job selling shit. By this time I was not only 15, but my body was that of a man in such a short period of time from the intensive weight training in my basement directed by Al Eisenhuth, I landed a job in a South Philly meat warehouse unloading the huge beef from trucks arriving from out west, that was later made famous by the Rocky Balboa movies. But this was the 1950s, long before Rocky, when there was no hint of any romantic endeavor for it was brutal work, paid a wage, though not enough for such hard work.

The trucks came in, one after another, filled with huge skinned animals, heavy dead animals hanging on hooks attached to an overhead metal rod the length of the truck allowing each huge piece of meat to be rolled out along its ridge before running out of the truck and into the warehouse on a similar metal overhead rod that connected to other rods with hanging meat in rows upon rows inside the meat warehouse.

Four of us laborers were assigned to each truck so emptying it would be quicker, mostly local south Philly guys, some older family men, some addicts of one sort or another, rarely a friendly one among any of them, as I soon found out attempting some humor. "We got a fuckin comic here," one said as the others laughed.

But they didn't laugh when I began putting my shoulder to the beef with legs pumping as if pushing a football blocking machine as the sound of overhead rollers could be heard all the way into the warehouse, and rather than stopping in the open warehouse door as we had been doing until a dozen or so piled up, then slowly pushed in; I would push mine directly into the warehouse, a good twenty-five yards or more where a butcher would take it from there, turn around and run back into the truck, repeating over and over till I single-handedly, in a short time, moved more beef than the other three put together, causing the foreman to bring the others inside leaving me to unload each truck alone.

The immediate problem: When, for any reason anyone from the loading docks had any problem, due to any reason, they were transferred inside to the production line where sliced meats were wrapped and sealed, standing for a long shift without a break with dozens of unattractive middle aged South Philly women, a transfer causing nine out of ten guys to walk off the job, mostly all saying as if scripted: " Fuck this shit," a few telling me they were going to wait in the parking lot to "Kick your ass," for screwing up "my job," but none really did wait around, and within a week the trucks did not even come in, being diverted to another facility up in north Philly, with me being transferred inside to the production line, and after just an hour, I walked off the job myself.

Chapter 25

Jobs, jobs: No problem in Philly in the 1950s; one of the main reasons Philadelphia was called a "blue collar town," for before I even returned to Green Valley Road, I had a new job.

I had stopped to get a sandwich and the guy working in the shop also lived in Delaware County and after a few shared laughs when relating the ending of my job an hour before he told me that Nabisco in Lansdowne was hiring laborers in their warehouse with Halloween and Christmas cookies coming in not just by the truck-loads, but caravans of trucks. The only problem, all the jobs were on the all-night shift, from nine till four in the morning.

And so right he was, for next day I was hired and with a dozen other workers of all ages we began moving thousands of orange and black boxes of the classic Nabisco holiday ginger-snap cookies from delivery pallets inside trucks filled right up to their roofs, and then stacking them right up to near the roof of the warehouse itself.

It wasn't bad; there were a lot of guys yelling, singing, telling jokes with a fun-filled comradery that was making the time go by faster than within silence; until.... Yea, a big until.

The foreman, whom we were all introduced to when taking the job, all of a sudden was not just satisfied with the great job we were all doing, began screaming for us to move faster, and "to shut the fuck up and just do your work. Don't talk, you all got that," he screamed. At that moment the atmosphere changed for the worse and went downhill after, as this crazy old bastard with white hair walked around telling us stories of how he was so tough, and how he "kicked the asses" of more employees that he could count. When one of the guys laughed, he actually walked over and smacked him upside the head, knocking him down upon one of the cookie pallets, then turned and said with a booming voice, "any other of you fucking guys want to challenge me."

At that point I could not hold back my laughter, with most of the other workers looking at me and joining me, until this brute of a foreman looked in their direction, them now lowering their heads as he walked over to me.

"You got a fucking problem, boy?" he said to me. "Yeah, I said, who the fuck so you think you are talking to guys making just two dollars and sixty cents an hour doing this stupid shit."

By this time, he was close enough to me to deliver a shot as he had the other guy; but I suppose when he looked at my powerfully build body he knew better.

"You are fucking fired," he screamed. "Get the fuck off the grounds right now," and within five seconds I was out of the warehouse walking back to my apartment where my new young wife had made me a nice meal, but after just several bites I excused myself from the table, gave her a kiss, and left, walking back to the warehouse that was only a few blocks away.

When I entered you could hear a pin drop as they say, for there was no longer any music as had been blasting earlier, and all the workers looked up not only in astonishment, but with smiles on their faces as I waved a brotherly arm at them as I walked directly toward the foreman who had such a confused look on his face as I approached with a big smile on my face with him surprisingly putting out a slightly trembling hand, a split second before I landed the first of my lightning fast punches to the side of his fat head with my right fist, followed by a pounding left fist into his stomach, followed by six punches thrown faster than the human eye can calculate, driving his huge tall body back further and further with each volley of hits till he fell backward to the ground with hundreds of the orange and black ginger snap cookie boxes from high above fell onto him, now covering his entire body beneath, as if buried in Nabisco's holiday cookies.

At that point you would think I won the Superbowl, before it was invented; all the guys yelling and laughing and screaming as I simply walked out in the direction from which I entered. The end of another job.

Again, like Philly in these days, a few phone calls and a pal picked me up, along with a couple other guys and drove us thirty miles west to Downingtown Pennsylvania to a famous national food processing plant who were desperate to find employees, and when we all assembled in the warehouse for instructions it was a hoot; for most of us all new each other from sports, schools, neighborhoods, and the many Philadelphia tribes of guys stretching all the way to Wildwood New Jersey. A tough group of guys for any foreman to handle, no less educated on the art of cleaning and warehousing everything from the floor to the ceiling of this massive one-story plant.

One of the first lessons nearly ended in the foreman's death. He organized us into about four teams to go into the various freezers to scrape the movable conveyor belt that carried all the good food stuffs being frozen as he rode high above us in a fork-lift truck from freezer to freezer barking out mistakes many were making as we bent over with scrappers on our gloved but still nearly frozen hands; until my pal Ernie and I simply put a thick piece of medal across the exit and entrance doors of one of the freezers after all the guys had departed it as the foreman stayed behind to inspect.

Within a few minutes one of the guys retrieved two cases of beer from his truck and we sat around drinking, telling stories, and laughing our asses off, as time ticked by, and ticked by, and ticked by.

My having been through survival training in the military up in Tule Greenland had me checking my watch during this spontaneous party knowing how quickly one could be numbed enough to fall asleep in sub-freezing temperatures, death coming on faster than consciousness can register it. When I mentioned this, nearly everyone laughed and continued to throw down the beers and by now telling a string of dirty jokes; except my pal Ernie, an ex-U.S. Marine who knew sudden death first hand, who caught my eye just at the right time as we read each other's minds and just left the party, and swiftly walked the fifty yards to the freezer where we had trapped the foreman, pulling the medal pike off the handles and opening the door.

One step inside we froze, not from the cold, but from the sight of the foreman a good way up from our heads on the fork-lift, laying down, asleep, or dead? We had lost our sense of time out there at the beer party; but when we lowered the lift, he sat up and shook his head, as we both clapped before Ernie jumped up next to the foreman and drove the lift out of the freezer as a dazed foreman looked at us with a stare of utter confusion, as we asked him over and over, "what happened? Why did you not leave? Was the door stuck? With the guy shaking uncontrollably and his eyes more or less locked in place as if in shock. We soon had an ambulance taking him off to the hospital, that later ruled him perfectly ok but not enough to return to work.

When the new foreman arrived he spent time taking pictures of the entrance door to the freezer and questioned a dozen of us who all feinted ignorance of what happened before having all of us with broom or mop in our hands cleaning the entire warehouse floor, at one point calling out to us with the loud speaker of a bull-horn for all of us to assemble outside his office, for many of us had been engaged in a game of "hide and go seek," running and climbing up the 20 foot high stacks of folded boxes screaming, "Your it motherfucker," like children, half the guys married with young children themselves, laughing so loud, some screaming in pain from falling or rolling down onto the concrete floor. " one more violation of rules I will fire all of you, now get back to work and stop acting like children."

Which we did, at least for a while. All of us had walked by the one room with a locked door labeled "experimental kitchen," where people from around the world had sent their special cakes and pies to the company in hopes of a contract that would make them rich. Our mouths watered as we looked inside the windows at the displays in special glass encased containers, fixating on delicious looking special treats. On our first break after over an hour of cleaning the floors I convinced several of the guys to boost me on their shoulders allowing me to just get my fingers on the top of the outside wall, then pulling my body over the wall, for I had noticed there was no ceiling on the room, allowing me to drop down onto the floor before unlocking the door as guys came in and began to devour one delicious cake or pie after another until by the end of our break we were all laying outside on piles of boxes stuffed like kids at Halloween, moaning in pain, loud enough the new foreman found us.

We had committed a mortal sin in this business, and within five minutes we were all out in our vehicles heading back to Philly. We did not even make it a day, we were fired.

Chapter 26

Time takes everything and everybody in its path, like a title wave we not only don't see coming, but don't understand how it can destroy all we know.

We simply watch, as everything and everyone disappears, with just a few left to witness; "then," for there is no then, and never will be a then again in this time and place. All the noise from children playing, young mothers calling "dinner ready," music blasting into free happy air.

Some wake and walk to the bathroom to look in the mirror and shockingly, see only half a face, the stroke that only happens to all the old people, not us, dam, not us. Or that brief session in the doctor's office with the sun pouring into the room from above; white sterile walls, overhead lights that do not seem like lights, and the "I have some results that may upset you, your cancer has returned."

But on more subtle levels the red brick houses of Green Valley Road never really changed, just the faces that occupied those houses. This is true no matter where one lives, every neighborhood experiences this depletion of life as death takes those we know as if a slow-moving gray cloud rolls over the roof-tops and no longer do people emerge through the doors we recognize.

In the early years, crowds occupied the church as wedding bells rang out as cars decorated with streamers left the huge parking lots on both sides of the church with horns blasting and laughter filling the air; followed a few years later by crowds on more subdued occasions with baby baptisms, followed by more weddings, and then years later; the funerals began.

It may be universal, yes; but it is not personal till it happens to me, my block, my neighborhood, my people, when the music and laughter just ends, just ends, just ends. It is all so subjective and no previous understanding or knowledge of its inevitability gives any of us a protection from this brutal ending we all will eventually face. We face it alone.

I remember my own mother on Green Valley Road living alone in our home after my father died, having lived in this house since 1939 just after it was built, opening the large wood front door, just enough to glance out, as if she were afraid to be seen, and commenting, in a near whisper as if not wanting anyone to hear her: "Look at all the old people out there, where did they all come from?" Mom was 94 years old. She had lived in this house at 157 Green Valley Road since she was a young mother with me at three years old. This comes to all of us if we are "lucky" enough to live old. "Lucky?" me, as one guy who always expected to die young, and was pronounced dead twice, once in Ulan Batur Mongolia and once on the northwest corner of 79th and Amsterdam avenue in New York City, me. Maybe growing old is not so wonderful.

But the big question here is: who the hell could these people on Green Valley Road turn too in an attempt to understand the very nature of life and death, other than the spiritual explanations that always ended with such serious end-game finality clocked in the black colors of death; hey, maybe our spirits are being liberated, set free in a loving, pain free, debt free, universe.

Or, human life itself, is like other life all around us; the green leaves turn yellow or red in Autumn and fall to the ground, soon decaying into dust, then nothingness; or as animals in the forest or birds in the sky live, then die; so, we humans are no different. When researching and studying the life of the first emperor of China, this all-powerful confident man faced old age with a great deal of fear as he traveled his empire in his search of a secret to extent his life, and at one point in his utter frustration looked down at the droppings from a horse who had just shit and commented. "When I die, I will be nothing more than that horse's waste."

Funeral ceremonies at St Lawrence church were elaborate displays of not just ceremonial Catholic rituals with images and music and aromas of ancient burning incense that mystically transformed the atmosphere in which many were consciously transformed beyond this life, but attempts to increase one's belief in the hereafter, an existence beyond life itself. The problem for an agnostic is; has anyone ever come back to tell us about this here-after? On Green Valley Road back in the day, few questioned the gospel of the afterlife, mostly all fell into line.

That is why the Friday and Saturday Confession lines were so long, for deep down inside you did not want to die with unconfessed sins on your soul for fear you could end up in not just purgatory for long periods of time, but even land in hell for ever, for " all eternity" as we were taught. When the priest gave you absolution you walked out into the fresh air felling not just free, but clean of sin, sort of reborn, and now sufficiently cleansed to receive Holy Communion at Sunday Mass, itself mandatory less another sin committed. Hey, mass is where you were supposed to put money in the basket, no matter how young or old you were, why many heads lowered in embarrassment as the basket passed by them chest-high, many depositing cash others envelops with money inside along with the forms sent to them in the mail, later listed in the monthly parish newsletter listing all the streets with individual and family amounts of money given to the church that month. Everyone checked their names and amounts, mine always a zero, until a very amusing mistake. Twice a year the six month contributions were listed, bringing pride to those who were prideful. A row house neighbor two doors east of us, a Mr Fredericks, truly hated me and did his best to turn my parents against me, he and his wife more or less bribing them at times when they bought new furnishings for their house and gave my Mom and Dad the old shit, which Mom would say: " Expensive, do you know where it came from,?... meaning expensive downtown Philadelphia stores. Back to the listings; someone at the parish office made a mistake and listed the Fredericks money contributions under my name, and listed my total under there's,

"0." I do not remember laughing as hard as I did when my astonished mother showed me the six-month parish newsletter, her sympathies for the Fredericks quite obvious, and to my surprise, I think I detected a smile on my father's face as he turned his head away.

But the saddest stories about Green Valley Road are the ones left untold. Like all in life, time rules. What was a vibrant baby producing environment with laughter and the noises of children and teenagers playing all sorts of games like stick ball or step ball or touch football, eventually became as quiet as a ghost town as children married and moved away leaving parents alone with each other in empty houses and quiet streets, many experiencing loneliness for the first time in their adult lives.

The loneliness was most obvious at times such as Christmas Eve, a night that had for decades been filled with laughter, hugs, intimate family re-unions with loved ones coming home from as far away as California, Europe, and even Asia; just to be under that one roof to not just celebrate Christmas Eve, but deep down in the collective psychic to celebrate this sacred unique gem not just identified by the family name itself, but the one of a kind DNA they all carried from time of birth to death. This profound reality had little obvious recognition on this sacred eve, until years later, when it was all over, after time had taken parents and children alike, and all that was left of the family was the name itself, with no laughter, loud happy voices, children running and screaming, and older ones sitting quietly in the shadows, un-noticed, as their smiles hid the dreaded reality they were unwillingly contemplating, that this day's happiness and laughter was only an unrecorded, never to be again moment, in the history of the universe.

Then it got worse as spouses died off, leaving the surviving husband or wife alone with only the four walls and memories of the past. When morning came a sense of dread would sometimes grip them with this reality of nothingness, as though they were no longer even part of life itself. "What am I supposed to do for the rest of the day?" was not just painful but too embarrassing to even relate to anyone. A trip to the store would temporarily break one of this for a few hours, but the return to the empty four walls would have this once beautiful love-filled home feel more like a prison, but with no other human being to converse with, an emptiness in the pit of their stomach that just wanted to scream out, to cry out, "Please, someone come and see me, talk to me, make me laugh before I cry some more." Even the trip to the store became painful, just for the fact that they had to return to Green Valley Road that no longer gives them any love or comfort. That feeling at noon after eating lunch. "What am I to do for the rest of the day," a refrain repeated and repeated day in and day out, month in and month out, year in and year out, till it all ends, on Green Valley Road.